## *"Turn on the lights," Sam told Joe.*

Joe flipped up three light switches. The overhead fluorescent lights flickered momentarily, then died out. Joe worked the switches up and down a few times, but the lights refused to come on.

"Why did that happen?" Sam asked David.

"Uh, well . . ." David seemed hesitant, maybe even scared. "There could be an electrical problem."

"There has to be an electrical problem," Joe stated firmly. "Because there's no ghost in here. Got it? No ghost. It's impossible!"

Something crashed, a loud metallic clang.

Everyone froze. This was followed by a hollow knocking sound, similar to a horse's hooves clattering on pavement.

Sam felt a queasy sensation rise up from her stomach and move through her chest until it clutched at her throat. She realized this sensation was Pure Terror. In a raspy voice she managed to say, "What was that?"

# Other books in the
# **WiSHBONE**™ Mysteries series:

*The Treasure of Skeleton Reef*

*The Haunted Clubhouse*

*Riddle of the Wayward Books*

*Tale of the Missing Mascot*

*The Stolen Trophy\**

*The Maltese Dog\**

*Drive-in of Doom\**

*coming soon

# WISHBONE Mysteries

# TALE OF THE MISSING MASCOT

## by Alexander Steele

WISHBONE™ created by Rick Duffield

**Big Red Chair Books**™, *A Division of **Lyrick Publishing***™

This book is a work of fiction. The characters, incidents, and dialogues are products of the author's imagination and are not to be construed as real. Any resemblance to actual events or persons, living or dead, is entirely coincidental.

 **Big Red Chair Books**™, *A Division of **Lyrick Publishing**™*
300 E. Bethany Drive, Allen, Texas 75002

©1998 Big Feats! Entertainment

Edited by Pam Pollack

Copy edited by Jonathon Brodman

Cover concept and design by Lyle Miller

Interior illustrations by Genevieve Meek

**Wishbone** photograph by Carol Kaelson

Library of Congress Catalog Card Number: 97-74835

ISBN: 1-57064-283-4

First printing: January 1998

10  9  8  7  6  5  4  3  2  1

Printed in the United States of America

To my parents,
who first allowed me to be a kid

# FROM THE BIG RED CHAIR . . .

Oh . . . hi! Wishbone here. You caught me right in the middle of some of my favorite things—books. Let me welcome you to the WISHBONE MYSTERIES. In each story, I help my human friends solve a puzzling mystery. In *TALE OF THE MISSING MASCOT*, my good friend Sam and I investigate a mystery involving a mascot head that is stolen right from under everyone's nose.

The story takes place early in the school year, before the events that you'll see in the second season of my WISHBONE television show. In this story, Joe is fourteen, and he and his friends are in the eighth grade. Like me, they are always ready for adventure . . . and a good mystery.

You're in for a real treat, so pull up a chair and a snack and sink your teeth into *TALE OF THE MISSING MASCOT*.

# Chapter One

Fans on either side of the football field sprang to their feet.

"Hey, I can't see!" Wishbone shouted, his vision suddenly blocked by the human bodies in front of him. "Why do people always have to be so big?"

The Jack Russell terrier managed to find a sight-line down to the field. He saw a boy in the blue-and-gold uniform of Sequoyah Middle School streaking after a long pass. Wishbone felt his heart pounding as fast as the boy's cleats.

"Come on, come on, come on!" he whispered tensely. Even though Wishbone did not attend Sequoyah, he was one of the school's most loyal fans.

As the Sequoyah player kept his eyes on the ball, a player in the blue-and-gray uniform of Glenview Middle School raced right at his heels.

"Just pretend you're playing catch with a stick!" Wishbone urged. "It works for me every time!"

The pass was coming. Awfully high, though. The Sequoyah player leaped into the air. Grabbed at the ball. The next second the Glenview player plowed his shoulder pads into the receiver's body, and both players went crashing to the ground. And the ball bounced away.

Moans of disappointment drifted from the Sequoyah side of the stands. "Nice try, anyway!" Wishbone called to the receiver, as people returned to their seats.

"Ouch, that one hurt," Samantha Kepler said, sitting on the bench beside Wishbone. Sam was an outgoing, fourteen-year-old girl with silky blond hair and hazel eyes. She had many talents, but Wishbone felt her greatest trait was her willingness to lend a hand to someone in need. Her hand was also especially good at finding just the right spot to scratch behind his ears.

"The quarterback didn't put enough spiral into the pass," David Barnes said. "Without spiral, you've got no control." David had curly black hair and curious brown eyes. He was a deep thinker, with a special talent for tinkering with things mechanical. A trip to David's workshop was always a stimulating experience for Wishbone.

"It'll take a miracle to win this one," Joe Talbot said. He had brown hair that he combed back, and an athletic body. Though Joe didn't play on the football team, he was one of Sequoyah's top basketball players. Wishbone lived with Joe, and he considered the boy his very best friend in the entire world.

Wishbone attended every school football game with his human companions Joe, David, and Sam, all of whom *did* attend Sequoyah. The dog loved football, and this afternoon was certainly a perfect afternoon for the sport. The sky was a pure deep blue, and there was just a hint of briskness in the early October air. Wishbone thought he also noticed a scent of popcorn somewhere in his vicinity.

"If you ask me," Wishbone told his companions, "I think that might have been 'pass interference.' Don't you agree?"

No one answered.

*Okay, ignore me,* Wishbone thought. *Just because you're a dog, people think you don't know the first thing about football.*

"You're going down, Sequoyah!" Wishbone heard a nearby voice cry out.

"Way down!" another voice cried.

"Way, way down!" a third voice added.

Wishbone was surprised to hear this kind of taunt on the home-team side of the bleachers. Looking back several rows, he had no trouble picking out the shouters. They were three husky boys, each with a buzz cut and the scarlet jacket of Jefferson, another middle school in the area and Sequoyah's biggest rival.

"See those guys behind us?" Sam said, nudging Joe. "They're Jefferson football players, aren't they?"

Joe stole a glance at the boys, then said, "That's right. We play Jefferson next week, so I guess they're putting in an appearance today to intimidate our team. A little psychological warfare, you might call it."

"Is that really necessary?" Sam asked.

"They must be doing something right," David said with a shrug. "So far this year, the Jefferson Bobcats have beat all of their opponents by at least thirty points. In football, the killer instinct pays off."

Hearing the clash of padded bodies, Wishbone returned his gaze to the game. Sequoyah tried a rough-and-tumble fullback run up the middle, but Glenview stopped it cold.

Wishbone shifted on the bench. *Hmm . . . things are looking grim. We're down by six, and it's fourth down late in the fourth quarter. It ain't over till it's over, though. Winning is still a possibility. Maybe we should call a time-out and figure out just the right play.*

The Sequoyah quarterback signaled a time-out. Then he hustled over to the sideline to talk with his coach. Right away, the six Sequoyah cheerleaders ran onto the field.

"Let's go! Let's go!" Wishbone barked. He hoped the cheerleaders would get the Sequoyah fans charged up enough to jolt their team toward victory. From the looks of it, they had enough energy to light up the entire town.

As the cheerleaders lined up in formation, Wishbone saw them being joined by the Sequoyah mascot, the Bulldog. The cheerleaders looked great in their matching outfits, but the Bulldog was another story. It was really just a student dressed in a worn-out brown Bulldog costume. The ears drooped, a few teeth were missing, and one of the eyes seemed as if it was about to fall off any second.

*What they really need down there,* Wishbone thought, *is a dashingly handsome Jack Russell terrier, maybe white, with a few well-selected spots of brown and black. Someone like . . . oh . . . I don't know—me. That other fellow, well, let's just say he's a poor excuse for a canine.*

Sam watched the mascot and decided that something needed to be done. "That Bulldog costume is so old it's embarrassing," she told her friends. "It bothers me every time I see it."

"It seems to get worse every game," Joe agreed.

"I'll bet the school bought it before we were even born," David remarked. "Personally, I think it's time the Bulldog started considering retirement."

The cheerleaders swung into their cheer. In perfect unison, they shook their pompoms in a well-rehearsed pattern, all the while shouting:

*"We are the Bulldogs! We are the Bulldogs!*
*We've got sharp teeth that bite and pierce,*
*So ya better watch out*
*'Cause weee're sooo FIERCE!"*

On the final word, the cheerleaders gestured at the Bulldog, who then clawed at the air with a ferocious swipe—or at least it was supposed to be ferocious. To Sam, the movement looked more as if the Bulldog were swatting a fly while he was half asleep.

Sam heard a burst of laughter behind her. She didn't have to look back to know it was the rowdy Jefferson boys.

As the cheerleaders yelled "Gooo, Bulldogs!," the mascot ran toward one end of the stands, waving his paws weakly over his head. The Jefferson boys continued laughing, and Sam noticed the laughter was spreading.

11

A few Sequoyah fans were now chuckling at the mascot, as well. Again the cheerleaders yelled, "Gooo, Bulldogs!," as the mascot ran toward the other end of the stands. When the mascot tripped just a little bit, the laughter grew even louder.

"Poor Bulldog," David said after a sigh.

"Yeah," Sam said, her brow furrowed with worry. The Bulldog, Sam thought, was supposed to be a humorous character, but not one to be made fun of. The way she saw it, the mascot played an important role in boosting the school spirit for both fans and the team. And a school without spirit was like an ice-cream cone without the cone. Maybe the principal could be talked into ordering a new Bulldog costume. But then it probably wouldn't arrive until after football season was long gone. Something had to be done sooner. But what?

The game resumed, but the situation did not improve for Sequoyah. When the final buzzer sounded five minutes later, Glenview had won the game by a lead of thirteen. The players walked off the field, and the fans began clomping their way out of the bleachers. Sam watched the Bulldog. He was trudging off the field, shamefully, it seemed, far behind the cheerleaders.

"I guess that's it," David said. "Ready to go?"

When Sam caught sight of the Bulldog's sagging eye, she was suddenly seized with an idea. She jumped to her feet and said, "Come on. We've got to talk to the Bulldog!"

With Joe, David, and Wishbone following, Sam ran down row after row of seats until she stepped onto the grassy stretch of football field.

"Hey, Bulldog!" Sam called. "Wait up!"

The Bulldog turned around. At close range, his drooping ears, missing teeth, and dangling eye looked even more pathetic.

"Can I talk with you a second?" Sam said as she hurried over to the mascot.

The Bulldog hesitated, as if uncertain whether he wanted a conversation right now. Finally, he reached up his furry paws and pulled off the dilapidated head.

Sam was now face to face with Toby O'Shaughnessy, the student who played the Bulldog. He was a skinny boy with freckles, shiny braces on his teeth, and a mop of unruly hair. Toby was a smart kid, but talking to him wasn't always easy because he tended to be on the shy side.

By this time, Sam's friends had caught up with her. "Great job this afternoon," Sam told Toby. "You're always out there giving it your best."

13

"Absolutely," Joe agreed.

"And it's a lot of fun watching you," David added.

Toby muttered something in reply.

"Excuse me?" Sam said, not understanding the words.

"I'm afraid it's *too* much fun," Toby said, speaking a bit louder. "People were laughing at me today."

"Hey, it's a football game," David said, trying to be helpful. "People are supposed to . . . you know . . . let loose a little."

Sam saw Amanda give a big wave as she headed their way.

"Hi, there, everyone," Amanda said as she joined the group. "Tough game, huh? Listen, Toby, if you don't mind, I've got some advice for you."

Amanda Hollings was a self-assured girl with a flowing mane of black hair. She was given to overly dramatic gestures, which was probably because she considered herself a terrific actress. Sam liked Amanda, even though the girl was sometimes a bit much.

"What's your advice?" Toby asked, seeming as if he would rather not hear it.

"What you need to do," Amanda said, already gesturing, "is start acting a lot more, well, you know . . ."

"Vicious?" Toby suggested.

"Exactly!" Amanda said. "For example, you should really work those teeth, as if you're ready to chomp at anyone who passes by. Also, when you wave your hands in the air, you should put some real energy into it. And maybe, every now and then, you should give a big, bold, bulldogish lunge!" As Amanda emphasized each of these points with the appropriate physical

14

gesture, Toby stepped back, as if he feared physical harm.

"That's good advice," Sam said, putting a comforting hand on Toby's shoulder. "But, in my opinion, Toby's not really the one to blame here."

"He's not?" Amanda asked.

"I'm not?" Toby echoed.

"No," Sam said, easing the Bulldog head out of Toby's hands. "The real problem here isn't Toby, it's the costume. Especially this head."

"What *happened* to that head?" Wishbone wondered as he looked up at it. "Did the Bulldog play football a few years in the big leagues without a helmet?"

"It does look a bit pitiful," Toby said, examining the head as if for the first time.

"Yes, it does," Sam said. "But it's nothing some glue and a little imagination can't fix. Here's what I propose. Let me take the Bulldog head home with me, and I'll have it looking like a dog-show champion in no time at all."

"Well, if anyone can do it," David said, "you're the one."

"This is true," Wishbone said, well aware of Sam's creative abilities.

"He'll need the head back by next Saturday," Joe told Sam. "Remember, that's the big game with Jefferson."

"No problem," Sam replied.

"Toby still needs to put a lot more gusto into his

performance," Amanda said, refusing to let Toby off the hook. "The part of the Bulldog requires an actor of tremendous commitment."

"We know, Amanda," Sam said. "But, Toby, once you see how I've fixed up this head, I guarantee it's going to inspire you into a viciousness you never dreamed of. Now, on to other matters. Do either of you need a ride home?"

"I was planning to walk," Amanda answered.

"Me, too," Toby said.

"My mom is driving over to pick up me, Sam, David, and Wishbone," Joe said. "And I think she's planning on taking us to Pepper Pete's for some after-game pizza. Why don't you two call your parents and ask if you can come along?"

"Pizza! Yes!" Wishbone cried, going into a little dance of joy. He noticed Amanda smiling down at him. Then he saw a terrified look on Toby's face. Wishbone spun around to see what was frightening him.

There stood the three Jefferson boys, their buzz cuts looking sharp enough to cut a paw on. One of the boys bent his head to the Bulldog head in Sam's hands. In a tone of mock politeness, he said, "Hello there, Mr. Bulldog. Next Saturday, please, oh, please, don't scare us too much!"

At that remark, the three Jefferson boys exploded with laughter.

# Chapter Two

*Just wait until next week,* Wishbone thought as he watched scenery fly by outside the car window. *Yeah, we'll show those Jefferson boys. We'll tear 'em from limb to limb. I guarantee it!*

Wishbone turned to Joe, in whose lap he was perched on the window side of the front seat. Wishbone thought Joe had a great smile, but the boy wasn't wearing it now. He seemed a little disappointed about losing the game. "They needed you on that field today," Wishbone told his pal. "But you'll get your chance to shine in a few weeks, when basketball season starts. Bet you can't wait for that, can you?"

"Do you think we have a chance against Jefferson next Saturday?" David asked Joe. Joe turned to his friend, who was sitting in the front seat between Joe and Ellen.

"Sure, we've got a chance," Joe said seriously. "But if we don't play our very best, it's about one chance in a million. That Jefferson team is just awesome this year."

"Just remember, winning's not everything," Ellen Talbot said from the driver's seat of her sport utility vehicle. Joe's mom was slim and had thick brown hair that fell to her shoulders. She was considered by Wishbone to be the ideal mother—wise, warm-hearted, and a superior chef.

Wishbone turned to check out the conversation in the backseat. Sam occupied the middle space, holding the Bulldog head on her lap. Toby and Amanda sat on either side of her. Sam was studying the head, and Wishbone knew she was already planning how to perform the repair job. Amanda was still gesturing and giving Toby advice on how to better play the role of Bulldog.

". . . if you could find a way to work in some real menacing growls," Amanda was saying. "You know what I mean? They have to be loud, though."

Toby nodded, but Wishbone could see that the kid was becoming more and more annoyed by Amanda's insistent advice. Toby sat there, stretching a rubber band in both directions, pulling it tauter and tauter.

*Man, that Amanda is like a dog with a bone*, Wishbone thought.

"Grrrr!" Amanda growled, baring her teeth.

The rubber band snapped.

Ellen stopped at a light, and Wishbone could see they were at the intersection just before Pepper Pete's. "Oh, we're getting close," Wishbone said, his tail tapping the back of the seat with anticipation. "I can almost smell that delicious pizza baking in the oven—the crispy crust, the flowing tomato sauce, the layer of melted cheese . . . all topped by the pizzazz of pepperoni! Yum!"

18

Sam ran a finger along one of the Bulldog's teeth, wondering what she could use to replace the missing ones. Meanwhile, Ellen steered the car into the parking lot right next to Pepper Pete's, then parked. When Ellen pushed a button, Sam watched as all the windows whirred their way up. As seat belts were unbuckled and everyone started to get out of the car, Sam set the Bulldog head on the backseat.

Sam climbed out of the forest-green sport utility vehicle and shut her door. Walking toward Ellen, who was a few steps away, Sam said, "Mrs. Talbot, could you please lock up? I don't want to risk having anything happen to the Bulldog head."

"Oh, don't worry," Ellen told Sam. "I always lock up. You see, I have one of these devices that allows me to lock the car by pushing a button on my key."

Ellen showed Sam the car key. At the end of it was a black piece of plastic with a button. Just as Ellen was about to push the button, Sam said, "Wait." She suddenly noticed that Toby was just then climbing out on the car's far side. *What was he doing in there so long?* Sam wondered. *Finding a few more rubber bands to fidget with?*

Sam turned her attention back to Ellen's key. After Toby closed his door, Ellen pushed the button, and Sam heard a distant click. "All locked up," Ellen said, giving Sam a smile of reassurance.

Pepper Pete's was crowded and rattling with activity, as it usually was around five on a Saturday evening. About twenty minutes after placing their order, Sam and her friends were digging into a pair of large pepperoni pies. Sam was glad to see that Amanda was hungry enough to let the Bulldog issue rest for a while.

"Here you go, boy," Joe said, sliding half a pizza slice onto a plate on the floor. Sam watched Wishbone lunge into the pizza as if he had not eaten in several weeks.

"Hi, Dad," Sam called, seeing her father approach the table. As usual, there was a friendly twinkle in his eye. Mr. Kepler had recently bought Pepper Pete's and turned it into one of the most popular spots in town. Sam had helped liven up the interior decor, which featured brick walls, shiny black tables, and a rocking jukebox.

Everyone at the table said hello to Sam's dad. "Sorry I didn't greet all of you sooner," Mr. Kepler said, wiping his hands on an apron. "But I was busy in the kitchen. How did the game go?"

"Don't ask," Sam replied with a groan.

"Enough said," Mr. Kepler responded, with a sympathetic nod.

"Do you want some help?" Sam asked her dad.

"Uh, well, it *is* getting pretty busy," Mr. Kepler said, noticing several customers entering at once. "If you don't mind, that might be nice."

"Sure thing," Sam said, rising from the table.

Sam grabbed a pen, order pad, and two menus from up front. Then she approached two ladies who had just sat down together. They were fashionable women, both with frosted-blond hair and expensive-looking leather jackets. Numerous shopping bags lay next to them at the foot of their table.

"May I get you something to drink?" Sam said, stepping around the bags to set down the menus.

"Oh, we're not ready to make that decision yet," one of the ladies answered.

"I'll come back," Sam said cheerfully.

"Oh, miss!" a man called in Sam's direction.

Sam hurried to the table, which was occupied by a burly man with a bushy moustache. A stuffed laundry bag sat on the floor beside him, and Sam figured he had recently come from the nearby laundromat.

The man pointed to the large pizza in front of him. "I ordered a jumbo deep-dish pie with a double helping of onions, peppers, and anchovies," he said in a gruff voice. "But this pizza doesn't look very jumbo to me."

"That *is* the large size, sir," Sam said.

"But I ordered jumbo."

"Yes, but we don't have jumbo, sir. Large is as big as it gets in the deep dish."

"Well, this'll have to do, then," the man said. He reached out a hand for a piece of his pie.

Sam saw one of the fashionable ladies waving to her. "Yes, ma'am," Sam said, after hurrying back to their table. "Have you decided what you want to drink yet?"

"No," one of the women said. "But there *is* something I wish to call your attention to."

"What's that?"

The lady arched her eyebrows. "There is a dog in this establishment. My friend and I do not like dogs."

"I'll mention it to the owner," Sam said politely. Then she moved away.

Sam stopped at the next table, where another newly arrived customer sat. He was a boy who looked to be around Sam's own age. Through his shaggy, dark hair, Sam spotted him wearing a single earring.

"Hi," Sam said.

"Hi," the boy said. Then he played a quick drum-roll on the tabletop with his fingers. "I'll try to be a little easier on you than some of your other customers. I'll take a small cheese pizza and an iced tea. That's a small pizza, not a jumbo. And, by the way, I don't mind dogs at all."

Sam chuckled, appreciating the humor. The boy smiled, showing a crooked front tooth.

After jotting down the order, Sam lingered at the table. "I don't think I've seen you in here before," she said.

"I've been here once or twice. I guess you weren't on duty. Do you work here much?"

"Only part-time. Mostly because my dad owns the place. I'm Sam, by the way."

"The name's Johnny. And we've got something in common. I help out with my dad's business, too."

"Where do you go to school?" Sam asked.

"Waitress, please," one of the fashionable ladies called.

Sam rolled her eyes. "Sorry. I'd better go."

"See ya," Johnny said.

Sam hurried back to the ladies.

"I believe we are prepared to order our drinks now," one of them told Sam. "And I see that dog is still in the dining room."

"Yes, and I'm enjoying myself tremendously," Wishbone said from his spot on the floor. He had been watching Sam's waitressing activities. As a rule, the dog's keen eyes and ears picked up practically everything around him.

Soon things settled down in the restaurant, and Sam returned to the table where her friends were sitting. Right around that time, Amanda went back to hounding Toby about his Bulldog performance. Wishbone watched the scene at the table above.

"Oh, I just thought of a fantastic idea!" Amanda told Toby. "Have you ever studied a real bulldog in action? *Really* studied one? Have you ever noticed the way— Toby, are you listening?"

Toby could take no more. He worked up the nerve to say, "Amanda, I . . . uh . . . I appreciate your concern. Really, I do. But maybe I don't think this Bulldog job is the single most important thing in the world!"

"Not important?" Amanda said, her eyes growing wide with shock. "Don't you . . . I mean . . . Oh, forget it. Just forget it. Fine. I won't utter another syllable about the Bulldog!" Amanda crossed her arms and looked away, obviously put off.

Immediately, Toby seemed sorry for his outburst. *This guy has had a really tough day,* Wishbone thought. *He looks like the last pooch left at the pound.*

*I think Sam is picking up on his feelings, too. Wait, she's about to do something.*

Sam clinked a spoon against her glass to catch the attention of everyone at the table. "Folks," she announced, lifting her glass in the air. "Toby, here, is always giving cheers for others, but I think he deserves one of his own—or maybe more of a toast. So, here's to Toby O'Shaughnessy, the greatest school mascot in the town of Oakdale!"

Ellen, Joe, and David lifted their glasses and, along with Sam, called out, "Here's to Toby O'Shaughnessy, the greatest school mascot in the town of Oakdale!" Wishbone threw in a congratulatory bark. But Wishbone noticed that Amanda did not participate in the toast. And, for some reason, poor Toby now looked as if he were about to be ill.

Sam hoped that she hadn't embarrassed Toby, and she did her best to guide the rest of the conversation away from the subject of the Bulldog. At any rate, the next half hour passed without any big event, except for Johnny's waving to Sam as he left the restaurant.

Finally, Ellen picked up her purse and said, "Well, it's just about six-thirty. Why don't I get us all home?"

Sunset tinted the sky as the group moved through the parking lot toward Ellen's car. Amanda walked swiftly ahead of the others. *Why is she in such a rush?* Sam wondered. Was Amanda afraid she would turn into a pumpkin at nightfall? Amanda reached the car ahead of the rest of the group. Sam watched

Ellen push the button on her car key to unlock the doors.

"How was that pizza?" Sam asked, as Wishbone trotted alongside her. When Wishbone looked up at Sam, she could have sworn she saw a contented smile on his lips.

"I'll tell my dad you send your compliments," Sam joked.

Soon Sam climbed into the backseat beside Amanda, who was already in place. Toby slid in next to Sam, while everyone else piled into the front seat.

"Everybody buckle up," Ellen said, as she inserted her key into the ignition.

Sam pulled the seat belt around her waist and was just about to fasten it when she realized something. She was sitting right where she had placed the Bulldog head before getting out of the car. But it wasn't there.

Sam glanced to her right at Amanda, then glanced to her left at Toby. But neither one of the kids was holding the head, and there was no empty space on the seat. Sam checked the floor in front of her. Then she turned to look in the storage compartment behind the backseat. Strangely, the head was nowhere to be seen.

The vehicle's engine rumbled to life. Sam felt a flicker of panic.

"Hey, guys," Sam called to the people in the front seat, "do you have the Bulldog head up there?"

"No," Joe said, turning around. "I thought you left it in back."

"I did. But it's not here."

Both David and Wishbone turned around. "What do you mean, it's not there?" David asked.

"I mean, the Bulldog's head isn't in the backseat," Sam said, hearing the tenseness in her voice. "It isn't in the storage area, either. So if it's not in the front seat, somebody must have stolen it!"

# Chapter Three

Sam felt her face flush with heat. She took a breath, trying to calm down. The head wasn't really gone, she told herself. She was probably just having one of those little scares that would turn out to be nothing a minute later.

"Sam," Ellen said, looking back with concern, "are you positive the Bulldog head isn't there?"

"All I can say is that I don't see it," Sam replied.

Ellen shut off the engine. "Why don't we all get out of the car just to make sure," she advised.

The doors were opened and everyone, including Wishbone, climbed out. Sam looked over the vehicle's entire interior—front seat, backseat, and storage compartment. Except for a box of tissues, a stray candy wrapper, Ellen's purse, and the spare tire in the back, the car was completely empty.

"There's no way that thing's in the car," David said, looking through one of the opened doors. "It would be kind of hard to miss a big brown Bulldog head, wouldn't it?"

The situation was so baffling it gave Sam the

creeps. "I know for a fact I left it sitting on the backseat right before Mrs. Talbot locked the car," she said. "And I know for a fact it wasn't here right after she unlocked the car."

"Hmm . . ." Ellen said, slowly shaking her head. "I hate to say it, but maybe the Bulldog head *was* stolen."

"But how could it have been?" Sam asked with disbelief. "I heard the locks click, and I saw that every window was all the way up before we even got out!"

"Let's test the locks," David suggested. "Mrs. Talbot, could you push that remote lock button?"

Ellen pushed the locking mechanism on her key, and Sam heard a click. David went around the car, attempting to open every door by hand. Then he announced, "Yes, these doors are definitely locked."

Toby muttered something, and Joe asked him to repeat it. "Maybe somebody broke into the car," Toby said, a bit louder.

"It's not so easy to break into a car," David said, running his eyes over the vehicle's forest-green exterior. "Not unless you smash a window or do some real damage. But we can see there's not sign of a break-in anywhere. No scratches, no marks—nothing. This vehicle is in mint condition."

"And this car is an Explorer," Ellen pointed out. "The manufacturer claims it's one of the most secure automobiles you can buy."

Amanda spoke up. "Mrs. Talbot, do you have an extra set of keys someone could have used?"

"I have one extra set of keys," Ellen replied. "But I keep it locked in a box at home. And Joe is the only one who knows about it."

"And I don't think I've ever touched those keys," Joe added.

Amanda shrugged. "Just thought I'd ask."

As the sunset deepened into darkness, Sam felt a terrible sense of helpless frustration. "It seems *impossible* that somebody could have stolen that head!" she exclaimed. "Yet, that must be what happened. But who would do such a thing? And *how* did they do it? And why did I have to get mixed up with that dog head in the first place? I feel like this is all my fault!"

Ellen put a comforting arm around Sam. "I know you're upset. But there has to be a reasonable explanation for this, and hopefully we'll find it. Right now, let's just go home."

On the ride home, Wishbone didn't really know what to say about the missing mascot head, so he just kept quiet. After Ellen dropped off Toby and Amanda, the rest of the group got out at the Talbot house. Wishbone followed Sam, Joe, and David toward the living room, while Ellen went to the kitchen. Wishbone thought he had the nicest home on the block. The floors and wall paneling were built of handsome wood, and there were plenty of comfy places to lounge.

As soon as Wishbone stepped into the living room, he heard the refrigerator open. Ordinarily, he would have been at the fridge almost before the light came on, but he noticed Sam sitting on the couch, wearing a sad expression. *Poor Sam,* he thought. *She's always trying to help out other people, but this time it got her into a sticky predicament.*

He jumped up beside Sam and nestled against her leg. "Fear not," Wishbone said reassuringly. "No matter how tough the problem, I'm here for assistance."

Sam smiled at Wishbone and stroked his head.

A knock sounded at the front door, and Joe went to answer it. A moment later, he returned with Wanda Gilmore, the Talbots' next-door neighbor. She was president of the Oakdale Historical Society. Wanda was tall, thin, and one of the more unusual humans Wishbone knew. She wore a purple jumpsuit that was as loud as her personality.

"Hello, everybody," Wanda said, twirling a gauzy purple scarf that was draped around her neck. "I saw the whole gang get out of the car, so I figured I'd see what all of you were up to. I can't stay very long, though. I've got a date with a fireman. We struck up a conversation in the grocery store the other day and, well, sparks just seemed to fly. So what are you folks doing tonight?"

"Not much," Joe said in a glum tone. "We had sort of a problem this evening."

Wanda sat in a chair, a worried look crossing her face. "Oh, really. Why, tell me what happened."

As Ellen brought in bowls of ice cream from the kitchen, Joe and David sat down and explained all the details of the missing mascot head to Wanda. Sam just listened, slowly eating her ice cream. Wishbone savored the rich chocolatey aroma coming from her bowl. He really wanted to request a few licks, but he resisted. He figured Sam needed the treat now more than he did.

Ellen sat in a large gray chair. "Any ideas what might have happened?" she asked Wanda when the story was done.

Wanda twirled her scarf as she thought things over. "Sam wanted to have that Bulldog head fixed up in time for the game with Jefferson next week, right?"

Sam nodded in response.

"Well," Wanda said, "as a matter of fact, I do have an idea. It's a bit otherworldy, but then this is a very mysterious situation."

*Oh, brother,* Wishbone thought. *Knowing Wanda, I've got a feeling this'll be a doozy.*

Wanda began. "One of my friends in the historical society has a son who attends Jefferson Middle School. And the son says there is such a thing as the Jefferson Ghost."

*A ghost? Uh-huh, I'm listening.*

"According to the tale," Wanda continued, "it's the ghost of a Jefferson teacher who passed away a number of years ago. Apparently, this man loved Jefferson so dearly that he now and then haunts Jefferson sporting events. It's said that this ghost may even be responsible for Jefferson's recent winning streak."

"What might this ghost have to do with the Bulldog?" Joe asked.

"I'm getting to that," Wanda said. "Now, according to the rumors, this ghost haunts both home and away games. That means he knows how to fly around or take the bus—or however it is that a ghost travels. Well, maybe some kind of ESP told that ghost the Bulldog head was sitting in Ellen's car. And, most likely, the ghost would know that Jefferson plays a football game against Sequoyah next week. Also, as you may know, there is a tradition of schools stealing the mascot of a rival school before a big game."

"Miss Gilmore, what are you saying?" David said doubtfully. "That the ghost magically entered the car and made off with the Bulldog's head?"

"Yes, that is exactly what I'm saying," Wanda replied, pulling off her scarf and floating it eerily in the air. "You might call it a demonstration of 'school spirit'—in more ways than one."

*Yeah, right,* Wishbone thought. *A ghost slithered into the car and then just drifted away with the big Bulldog head. Hey, maybe he's planning to wear it for Halloween.*

"I'm only half serious, mind you," Wanda said, returning the scarf to her neck. "But I do believe in supernatural happenings, and, well, who knows? Maybe it's worth looking into."

"Maybe so," Joe said halfheartedly. Wishbone could see that no one in the room was paying any serious attention to the ghost story.

"You know what this missing-mascot situation reminds me of?" Ellen asked everyone.

"Tell us," Wishbone said eagerly. He knew Ellen would have something interesting to say. In addition to being a librarian, she was an aspiring writer and the biggest book lover Wishbone knew—with the possible exception of himself.

"A locked-room mystery," Ellen said.

"What's that?" Sam asked, leaning forward.

"A locked-room mystery!" Wishbone cried out. "Of course. That's *exactly* what this is like. You see, Sam, a locked-room mystery is—"

34

"A locked-room mystery," Ellen explained, "is a type of crime that used to appear in a lot of detective novels. Some people consider it the ultimate mystery puzzle."

*That's what I was about to say—if anyone would bother to listen to me,* Wishbone thought.

"But I still don't understand what a locked-room mystery is," Sam said.

"It usually works like this," Ellen said. "A murdered person is found alone inside a room that's completely locked from the inside. In other words, all the doors and windows are locked in such a way that they could only have been fastened by a person who was *inside* the room. The people who discover the body usually have to break the door down to get in."

"But that's impossible," David said. "How could the criminal commit the murder and then escape, leaving the room completely locked behind?"

Ellen smiled mischievously. "That's what makes a locked-room mystery so puzzling. It seems absolutely impossible to solve. But then, in the end, there's always a logical explanation."

"You're right, Mrs. Talbot," Sam said thoughtfully. "It's very similar to our situation today. We found the car completely locked, and you're the only one who had a key. And there was no sign of a break-in. Yet, incredible as it seems, somehow that Bulldog head was stolen. I guess you might call it a locked-car mystery."

"Carr!" Ellen exclaimed.

"That's right," Sam said. "Just like the car."

"No," Ellen said. "I just remembered—there's a

certain author who's famous for his locked-room mysteries. He's considered the grandmaster of that kind of story. And, believe it or not, his name is John Dickson Carr!"

"What a cool coincidence," David remarked.

"Hey, Mom!" Joe said, jumping to his feet. "Do you think we might have any of John Dickson Carr's books in Dad's mystery-book collection?"

"Good thinking!" Wishbone said. Not long ago, he and Joe had found a cardboard box in their attic that turned out to be a treasure chest of mystery books that had belonged to Joe's dad. Steve Talbot had passed away from a rare blood disorder when Joe was only six, but Wishbone knew that Joe felt closer to his dad whenever he read one of those mysteries.

"I think there might be," Ellen told Joe. "Why don't you go check?"

As Joe hurried from the room, Wanda said, "I've never heard of John Dickson Carr."

Wishbone was about to fill her in, but then he decided to let Ellen do it. She *was* the librarian, after all.

"John Dickson Carr isn't read that much anymore," Ellen informed the group. "But he was very popular in the 1930s and 1940s. He wrote tons of books, and almost every one of them is some sort of locked-room mystery. I know several mystery buffs who consider him their favorite mystery writer."

"Well, live and learn," Wanda said.

After several minutes, Joe returned, holding a paperback book over his head. "Eureka! This novel is called *The Hollow Man,* and it's by none other than John Dickson Carr!"

"Oh, yes, I remember that book," Ellen said with a look of fondness. "Steve's uncle brought it to him from England. In fact, American editions of the book go by a completely different title, *The Three Coffins.* That happens sometimes, where books have different titles in England and America."

"Can I borrow the book?" Sam asked Joe.

"Sure," Joe said, handing the book to Sam. "Be careful with it, though. It looks really old."

"Thanks," Sam said. "I can use all the help I can get figuring out what happened to that head."

Wishbone stood to get a better look at the paper-back. It was faded and dog-eared the way the best books often were. Across the cover, the shape of a person loomed in a spooky silhouette of black. Immediately, Wishbone's tail went wagging. He loved a good book almost as much as he loved a good meal and, well, life itself.

"You know," Wishbone told Sam, "I've got a feeling this book is going to be just the thing we need to solve this case. After all, who better to help with a locked-car mystery than John Dickson Carr?"

# Chapter Four

A lovely Sunday morning lingered in the neighborhood. Sunny but refreshingly cool. As white clouds floated through the sky, autumn leaves drifted to the ground and nobody seemed in much of a rush to get anywhere.

After breakfast, Wishbone had entertained himself around the neighborhood—wrestling with a Sunday newspaper, slumbering in a shady spot, and visiting with some local dogs at the corner oak tree. *Yes, sir,* Wishbone thought, *it's been a full morning of leisure, and I've worked up quite an appetite. If I'm not mistaken, it's time for brunch.*

Wishbone trotted up the front porch of the Talbot house. "Helllooo!" Wishbone called, giving a scratch at the door. "It's me, Wishbone. Yep, I'm right here—and guess what? I'm hungry."

There was no answer.

"Hey, it's me, Wishbone. Remember? Your trusty dog. Joe, I know you're doing some math homework. And Ellen, I know you're trying to write a short story for that magazine. But, come on, guys, this is something truly important!"

There was still no answer.

"Drat!" Wishbone said to himself. "I'm in serious need of something to eat. Not two hours from now, not twenty minutes from now. *Now!* Aha! Not to worry. I have the emergency-snack backup plan."

Wishbone trotted next door to Wanda's house. It was far more interesting than the average home, decorated with all sorts of fanciful shapes. It reminded Wishbone of the gingerbread house in the story *Hansel and Gretel.* Unfortunately for him, though, this place was not constructed of anything edible.

However, scattered around Wanda's front yard lay all sorts of fresh-dirt gardens. Wishbone always kept a ready supply of bones buried in the dirt. Wanda also kept some flowers planted in these gardens, but Wishbone allowed that because the flowers didn't get in his way too much.

Wishbone stepped into one of the gardens, put his nose to the ground, and began sniffing. He could find almost anything with his astonishing sense of smell. *Oh, bone, where are you? Aren't bones terrific? The next-best thing to food. Hard but not brittle, thick but not too big, smooth but not slippery. I just love the way that bony texture feels against my teeth. My mouth's already watering.*

A variety of scents filled Wishbone's nostrils—soil, worms, flowers, fallen leaves. But, for some reason, Wishbone wasn't picking up the one scent he was looking for—bone!

Wishbone was puzzled. He knew for a fact there was a bone buried in this particular garden. He decided to try another tactic. He selected the spot where he was almost certain the bone was located. Then he began digging. Particles of dirt went flying left and right as Wishbone sent his front paws into furious motion. Soon a nice-size hole took shape. But there was still no sign of bone. Wishbone went into his deep-digging technique, scooping out big chunks of dirt, one paw at a time. *Just a few more inches, and that bone should be right—*

Suddenly, Wishbone felt his paw being sucked into the ground. Startled, he pulled back.

"Whoa! What was that? An underground vacuum cleaner?"

Wishbone stuck his head inside the hole and detected two new scents. Bone and unfamiliar animal.

Cautiously, Wishbone lowered a paw into the hole. He could feel that a sideways tunnel had been created in the ground. He realized this tunnel was what had pulled his paw downward. He also realized that the tunnel had caused his bone to shift farther into the earth.

Reaching deep into the hole, Wishbone could just touch the bone. He made several attempts to scoop it upward, but the bone was too far out of reach.

"Hey, I don't like this one bit. This garden belongs to me, and I don't remember granting anyone else digging rights!"

Wishbone figured the tunnel must have been created by the mysterious animal. He glanced around for more clues to the animal's identity. Sure enough, he noticed a purple flower lying on the ground, its root totally eaten away. *So,* Wishbone wondered, *exactly who is this tunnel-digging, flower-chewing intruder?*

Wishbone turned his head, catching a sign of movement at the house. A window was shoved open, and Wanda stuck her head out.

"Wishbone," Wanda called out, "it's okay if you come in the yard, but I really don't want you in that flower garden! Do you understand?"

"Oh, let's not get into that silly garden argument again," Wishbone said. "We've got a real problem here!"

"No digging in my garden!" Wanda yelled. "Those are my flowers!"

"Well, those are my—"

Wanda shut the window.

*Humans,* Wishbone thought with frustration. *They never think the dog has anything important to say.*

Wishbone sat down to think matters through.

*Okay, some unknown creature has dug a tunnel in my*

*garden. Is that really so bad? Well, yes, it is. This tunnel has made one of my bones difficult to locate and impossible to reach. And wait, it gets worse. If there's one tunnel, there may be other tunnels. And that means, sooner or later, if not already,* all *of my bones might be permanently out of reach. Yes, this is definitely a problem. In fact, it's a crisis!*

Wishbone felt a bug land on his ear. Not feeling in a playful mood, he scratched it away.

*Take it easy. You've dealt with crisis situations before, and you'll find a way to deal with this one. Right now, what you need . . .*

Wishbone spotted Sam and David coming toward the Talbot house. Sam was on her bike, and David was walking. Sam gave Wishbone a wave and called out to him. Wishbone saw that she was carrying the John Dickson Carr book Joe had given her the day before.

*Oh, that's right,* Wishbone remembered. *We've got that strange locked-car situation to work on. Boy, there's mysteries every which way you turn in this town.*

"All right, let's go," Wishbone called as he ran up to Sam and David. "Time to get chewing on the case!"

# Chapter Five

Wishbone gnawed a piece of rawhide as he lay on the oval rug in the Talbot living room. A little chewing action helped him focus his thoughts—and he needed lots of focus. There was serious detective work to be done. The Jack Russell terrier enjoyed detective work, and with his high intelligence and extra-sharp senses, he considered himself especially adept at it.

Joe and David sat on the couch, while Sam occupied the gray chair. Wishbone was glad to see that Sam looked much less upset today.

"So," Joe said, squeezing a rubber ball in his hand, "did you find anything in *The Hollow Man* that might be helpful to our case?"

"I read just a few chapters," Sam said, holding up the paperback. "But before I set it down last night, I leafed through and noticed something very interesting about Chapter Seventeen."

David took a chomp out of an apple, then said, "You're not supposed to skip ahead in a mystery novel."

"I know," Sam said. "But this time it paid off.

Chapter Seventeen is titled 'The Locked-Room Lecture.' You see, the detective in this book is a grumpy professor named Dr. Gideon Fell, and he's had a lot of experience with locked-room mysteries. He's also kind of a funny character. He's always smoking a big cigar and muttering the words 'H'mf, ha.'"

"'H'mf, ha'?" Joe repeated with a chuckle.

"That's right," Sam said. "Anyway, in this chapter, Dr. Fell sits around a fire with several of his friends and analyzes all the possible solutions to a locked-room murder."

"To *any* locked-room murder?" David asked.

Sam nodded. "Yes. You see, Dr. Fell claims that every locked-room murder has to be a variation on one of his basic methods. As you know, we're examining theft, not murder. And we're talking about a locked car, not a locked room. But I still think some of these methods might be helpful to us."

"Let's hear what he has to say," Joe said.

"Yeah, this sounds interesting," David agreed.

"H'mf, ha," Wishbone said, looking up from his bone. "I'm ready when you are, Sam. All set to think my head off."

Sam delicately opened *The Hollow Man* to Chapter 17. The pages lay beneath her fingers, brittle and yellowed with age. Though she was still distressed about the missing Bulldog head, the book had fired her up with the challenge of solving the mystery. She hoped to get Joe and David fired up, as well.

"Method Number One," Sam announced. Then she read from the book: "'It is not murder, but a series of coincidences ending in an accident which looks like murder.'"

"What do you mean?" Joe asked.

"For example," Sam said, "and I'm putting this in my own words. Mr. X is alone inside a locked room. He accidentally trips on a snag in a rug, falls and cracks his head on a table, and dies. But everyone assumes he was murdered."

"You might call that a clumsy example," Joe said with a grin.

"And I don't really see how this one applies to our case," David mentioned.

"It doesn't," Sam said. "Not all of them do."

"What's the next one?" Joe asked.

"Method Number Two," Sam announced. Then again she read from the book. "'It is murder, but the victim is impelled to kill himself.'"

"Well, that's nice," David said. "Now, could you tell me what *impelled* means."

Sam smiled. "It's a fancy way of saying 'forced.' For example, Mr. X is alone inside a locked room. Then Mr. Z sends poisonous gas under the door that makes Mr. X go crazy and kill himself. Or a ghost enters the room—assuming that there *are* ghosts, and that they can walk through doors—and the ghost drives Mr. X to kill himself."

"Miss Gilmore would like that one," David commented. "But I don't think any of us believes in ghosts. And I don't see how gas could apply to our case."

"So let's also forget Method Number Two," Joe

said, switching the rubber ball to his other hand. "What's the next one?"

Sam could see that her friends were growing a little doubtful, but she figured that they would be hanging on her every word before this session was over. She noticed Wishbone was gnawing on a piece of rawhide as he watched her.

"Method Number Three," Sam announced. Then read: "'It is murder, by a mechanical device already planted in the room.' This one might sound a little silly. For example, Mr. X is alone inside a locked room. But someone has rigged a clock in there to shoot a bullet when it's wound. Mr. X winds the clock, and— *kapow!*—he gets shot dead."

Everyone chuckled.

"Ah, yes," Joe joked, "the old bullet-in-the-clock trick."

"Actually, this one could apply to our case," David observed. "You said 'a mechanical device already planted in the room.' Well, some people keep an extra key under one of the bumpers, as a backup in case they lock themselves out. Your mom didn't say anything about an extra key. But maybe she put one there some time ago and forgot about it."

Sam hadn't thought of that. "Nice thinking," she said. "If Mrs. Talbot does keep an extra key under the bumper, someone could have gotten it out and then used it on one of the doors."

"Let me check it out," Joe said.

He left the living room to go talk to his mother in the study and returned a minute later.

"It was a good theory, but it doesn't pan out.

Mom says she's positive she never put a hidden key under the bumper."

"Well, three strikes for Mr. Carr," David said. "Lucky this isn't baseball."

"Keep going," Joe told Sam, as he sat back down on the couch. "I have a feeling we're about to get a base hit any minute."

"Method Number Four," Sam announced. Then she read: "'It is suicide, which is intended to look like murder.'" She went on to explain. "This one might sound really silly. For example, Mr. X is alone inside a locked room. He stabs himself to death with an icicle, and then the icicle melts. Later, people find a body, but no weapon nearby, so they assume there's been a murder."

The kids had a good laugh at that theory.

"H'mf, ha," Joe declared. "How many people go around stabbing themselves with icicles?"

"H'mf, ha," David proclaimed. "Not many."

Sam chuckled as she turned a page in the book. "Stay with me. The plot is about to thicken."

"Shoot," David said. "But not with a wind-up clock."

Sam, Joe, and David cracked up again. When the laughter faded, Sam continued.

"Method Number Five," Sam announced. Then she read: "'It is murder which derives its problem from illusion and impersonation.'"

Joe and David exchanged a mutual, very confused look. "Hey, guys," Joe said humorously, "I'm all for finding that missing Bulldog head. But I have to say that this whole thing is starting to give me a major *head*ache!"

"Hang in there," David said. "We're starting to make some real *head*way!"

"I'm sure we can do it," Sam added, "if we all just put our *heads* together!"

At that, all three kids collapsed with laughter.

When they calmed themselves down, Sam said, "This one is so complicated that I'll just skip the example. But there's a very important idea in it. You see, in Method Number Five, the crime was committed some time *before* it was assumed to have been committed."

Joe bounced his ball. "Explain, please."

Sam paused a moment for effect. "Maybe," she said, "the Bulldog head was stolen *before* the car was actually locked."

Sam could tell that this theory had made the boys curious.

"How?" David asked, setting down his apple core.

Sam tucked her feet up underneath her. This part had gotten her so excited she could barely sleep the previous night. "I replayed a scene in my mind last night," she said. "Yesterday, we parked near Pepper Pete's. I set the head on the backseat, and everyone got out of the car."

Joe nodded, saying, "So far I'm with you."

Wishbone set down his rawhide and looked as if he was listening carefully to the conversation.

Sam continued, looking at Joe. "I walked over to your mom, who was several steps away from the car. She was just about to push the remote locking button on her key, but I told her to wait because Toby was still getting out on the car's far side. I remember wondering if he was looking for another rubber band to fidget with. Then Toby got out, and your mom locked the doors."

"I still don't see how the head could have been stolen before the doors were locked," David said.

"I wasn't watching Toby carefully," Sam said, "and I don't think anyone else was, either. Maybe— just maybe—Toby took the head out of the car with him and right away got rid of it somehow. Maybe he quickly slid it under another car, or something like that. And then the doors were locked. You see, in that case, the crime was committed *before*—not *after*—the doors were locked."

"Yeah, I guess it's possible," David admitted. "Very impressive, Sam. But why would Toby do that?"

"We can investigate that question later," Sam said. "The point is, Method Number Five is a possibility."

"Great!" Joe said enthusiastically. "Sam, you go straight to the head of the class. Let's move on to Method Number Six."

"Sorry to disappoint you," Sam said, "but Method Number Six is no help. In this one, Mr. Z kills Mr. X without actually entering the room—say, by shooting a bullet through a small opening, like a keyhole."

"So scratch Method Number Six," Joe said. "On to Method Number Seven."

"Method Number Seven is also promising," Sam said, turning a page in the book. "It's the exact opposite of Method Number Five. That is, the murder is committed at some point *after* the time it is assumed to have been committed."

Both boys leaned forward with interest.

"How?" David wondered.

"For example," Sam said, "Mr. Y and Mr. Z knock at the door of a locked room, but there's no answer. Mr. Z suspects foul play. So he breaks the lock, rushes into the room, then hurries out a few moments later with a horrified expression on his face. Mr. Y rushes in and sees that Mr. X has been murdered."

"I think I know what happened!" Joe cried, jumping up.

"The floor is yours," Sam said.

As he paced the room, Joe explained. "Mr. X was only sleeping in that locked room. Then Mr. Z broke the lock, rushed into the room, murdered Mr. X really quickly, and then he rushed out of the room as if he had just stumbled upon the murdered body!"

"Excellent!" Sam exclaimed.

"What do you think of that, boy?" Joe said, getting

off the couch and kneeling down to pet Wishbone a few times. The dog looked up at Joe with what Sam thought was admiration.

"I see," David said, rubbing his chin. "Yeah, the crime was committed *after* the time it was assumed to have taken place. Now, could that type of thing work with our case?"

"Yes, it could," Sam said with emphasis. "Last night I replayed another scene in my mind. We've just come out of Pepper Pete's. We're all heading for the car, but Amanda is way ahead of the rest of us. I remember wondering if she was afraid of turning into a pumpkin at nightfall. Then when Mrs. Talbot saw Amanda reach the car, she pushed the button to unlock the doors and Amanda climbed in."

"And at that time," David said with growing excitement, "Amanda could have disposed of the head—just

like Toby might have. In other words, she stole the head *after* the doors were unlocked."

"Precisely!" Sam said.

"You know," Joe said, going back to the couch, "there's still the possibility that someone just plain broke into the car. I know it's difficult to do, but it's possible."

"That's the last theory Dr. Gideon Fell explores in this chapter," Sam said. "A bunch of tricky ways a person could break into a locked room. Things like removing the door by its hinges, then putting it back in place. Let's just call breaking into the car Method Number Eight. And that's it."

"So how many of these methods might apply to our case?" David asked.

"Three," Sam replied. "Method Number Five— that's Toby. Method Number Seven—that's Amanda. And Method Number Eight—breaking in, which could be anybody."

"Not bad," Joe said, standing up again. "So what's next? I'm eager to get cracking on this case."

"Me, too," David said, as both he and Wishbone stood up. "What do we do, Sam?"

Sam was pleased to see that Joe and David were now plenty fired up. She closed the paperback and said, "I'm so glad you asked."

# Chapter Six

Wishbone noticed a doubtful look on Ellen's face. "You want to do *what?*" she asked. Ellen was sitting at her desk in the study, a stack of books beside her.

"We want to experiment on your car," Joe explained, with Sam, David, and Wishbone backing him up for support. "We want to see how difficult it would be for someone to break into it."

"Oh, come on, Ellen," Wishbone urged. "This'll really help us with Method Eight. It's only a car—just an overpriced hunk of metal that's fun to chase."

"We'll be extremely careful," David assured Ellen. "And I've got a lot of experience working on both my parents' cars. Besides, your car might be a lot less secure than you think it is. Isn't that something you would want to know?"

Ellen rolled a pen between her fingers. "As a matter of fact, it is. I mean, when I lock my car, I like to think it's . . . *locked*. Okay, give it a go."

"Terrific!" Sam said, leading the group out of the room.

Minutes later, the group was gathered around the Explorer, which was parked in the Talbots' driveway. As Joe and David pulled tools from a toolbox, Wishbone walked around the gigantic vehicle, trying to figure out where the experimentation might begin. "In my opinion," he told the others, "we should see if it's possible for someone to dig his way into the car from underneath. If I were a crook, that's the way I'd do it. Helllooo! Is anyone listening?"

"If it's all right," Sam said, tapping the car, "I'll leave this part to you guys."

"What are you going to do?" Joe asked.

"First," Sam said, "I want to visit a locksmith and get some professional advice on the ins and outs of breaking into a car—as part of Method Eight. Then I want to take a good look at the actual scene of the crime—as part of Methods Five and Seven, Toby and Amanda. I'll see you guys later."

Sam walked swiftly down the driveway. "Wait!" Wishbone called, trotting after her. "I can't let you do this alone, kid. The whole situation reeks of danger. Me—I love danger. I'm trained for danger—that is, as long as it's not too dangerous."

Soon Sam was pedaling her bike through the streets of Oakdale. She was pleased to see Wishbone galloping along beside her, his tongue panting with eagerness.

Sam admired the trees passing by, their leaves beginning to rust into autumnal shades of brown, gold, orange, and maroon. She found herself wondering why the leaves changed into such beautiful colors before they fell. Then she realized she was analyzing things more than she normally did, which was probably due to the fact that she was now playing the part of a detective. A sleuth had to sort through every little detail, never sure which odd piece might end up completing the puzzle. It was a whole new way of looking at the world, and Sam found it kind of fun.

After a long trip that took her to the outskirts of town, Sam brought her bike to a stop. She and Wishbone stood in front of a small shop with an overhead sign that read: ROSENBAUM & SON, LOCKSMITHS.

"Okay," Sam told Wishbone, "let's see what the locksmith has to say."

A bell attached to the front door jingled as Sam and Wishbone entered the shop. The place was decorated with doorknobs, lock cylinders, safes, padlocks, window gates, alarm systems, and every kind of key imaginable. A man stood behind a counter, working on some mechanism with a screwdriver and a pair of tweezers. He was a big robust fellow with a balding head. Sam guessed he was in his late forties.

"Howdy," the man said. "What can I help you with?"

"Are you Mr. Rosenbaum?" Sam said, removing her bike helmet.

"Last time I looked I was."

Sam noticed the man's fingers moving with the skill of a concert pianist. He kept working but seemed friendly enough to answer a few questions.

"I'm not here to buy anything," Sam said. "But,

56

you see, I'm trying to solve a sort of mysterious situation, and I thought you might be able to help me out."

"Mysterious?" Mr. Rosenbaum said with an interested glance. "Well, I'm no Sherlock, but I sure am a locksmith."

Sam smiled at the play on words. "I want to know how difficult it would be to break into a locked car, take something out of it, then relock the car, without leaving any kind of mark or damage."

Mr. Rosenbaum imitated a tough gangster voice. "Are you interested in taking up criminal ways? I don't recommend it, kiddo. Plenty of trouble down that road, see."

"Oh, no," Sam said, taking a liking to the man. "But I think someone might have stolen something out of my friend's mother's car."

Mr. Rosenbaum set down his tools and wiped his hands on a rag. "What kind of car is it?"

"Actually, it's a sport utility vehicle. An Explorer. A fairly new one."

"It would be very difficult," Mr. Rosenbaum said, leaning on the counter. "It used to be that you could just unbend a wire hanger, slip it over the window, catch it on the lock lip, and unlock the car. With a little patience, most anybody could do it. But nowadays the manufacturers make the locks a lot tougher to pick. You've got to slip a device past the weather stripping at the bottom of the window and find just the right spot in the door's interior. To make things even harder, the new cars have all sorts of things in the way: computerized wires, airbags, alarm systems—you name it. And it's said that the Explorer is one of the hardest cars on the market to break into."

"Could you break into one—that is, without smashing a window or leaving any marks?"

"*I* could, sure. But I'm a pro, and I've got all the proper equipment."

"What's the proper equipment?"

The locksmith reached under the counter and produced a canvas tool bag, from which he pulled a series of thin metal rods resembling car antennas. There was a total of eight, and the end of each rod curved or twisted into a unique shape. It almost looked to Sam as if eight shiny silver snakes were lying on the counter.

"Hey, let me take a look," Wishbone said, rising to his hind legs and scratching his paws against the counter. "This could be a crucial clue."

"Oh, sorry," Sam said, lifting Wishbone up to the counter's height for a better view. "I know you like to see everything yourself."

As Wishbone studied the unusual snakelike devices, Mr. Rosenbaum gave the dog's head a scratch. "These thingamajigs are made especially for picking car locks," Mr. Rosenbaum informed Sam. "You can buy them only if you're a licensed locksmith."

"They don't look very high-tech," Sam said.

"No, but they're the absolute best tools for the job."

"Why are there so many types?"

"Different types of rods work on different types of

cars. And I've got even more than the ones I'm showing you. I've also got a manual that tells me which type to use on which make of car. But even with the right equipment and the knowledge of how to use it, the job can still be very difficult. I'd say it would be just about impossible for an amateur to pick his way into an Explorer without leaving some sign of entry."

"How long would it take a professional to break in?"

"If you're really good, maybe five or ten minutes. If not, it could take up to an hour."

*Let's see,* Wishbone thought. *Yesterday we were in Pepper Pete's for about an hour and a half. I wonder if someone could have hired a locksmith to break into Ellen's car while we were eating.*

It seemed Sam was thinking the same thing. "If someone came to you," she asked Mr. Rosenbaum, "and said he or she wanted a car broken into, would you make them prove it was their car?"

"Absolutely," Mr. Rosenbaum said with a firm nod. "As soon as I got inside the car, I'd make the person show me the registration or insurance card in the glove department. Then I'd check the name on that card against their driver's license. If I wasn't satisfied the person owned the car or had a right to be in it, I'd call the police. Any other locksmith would do the same. We're very firm about this sort of thing."

*So much for that theory,* Wishbone thought. *But, then, someone might have at least* tried *to hire a locksmith for the job. And I believe this is the locksmith shop closest to Pepper Pete's.*

Again, Sam seemed to have the same thought. "By

any chance," she asked the locksmith, "did someone come in here late yesterday afternoon, asking you to break into a car?"

Mr. Rosenbaum shook his head. "Nope. I was out for a while, and my son watched the place, but he didn't mention anyone making that kind of request, either."

"Well, thank you very much," Sam said as she set Wishbone on the floor. "You've been very helpful."

Mr. Rosenbaum began returning the silver-toned snakes to their bag. Going back into his "gangster voice," he said, "Been a pleasure. See, I'm always glad to help a kid and a dog with a mystery."

Next, Sam traveled back across town and examined the crime scene. She sat astride her bike in the parking lot where Ellen had parked the Explorer the day before. Because it was Sunday, the area was now practically deserted. Wishbone waited faithfully at Sam's feet.

In light of the locksmith's revelations, Sam realized, it seemed more and more likely that either Toby or Amanda had stolen the Bulldog head. That was the only way the theft could have occurred without someone actually breaking into the car. So how, exactly, could one of them have pulled it off?

Sam studied the exact spot where Ellen had parked. As she did so, Sam visualized yesterday's events.

She remembered that Toby had gotten *out* of the car from the right door of the backseat, and that

Amanda had gotten *into* the car by way of the same door. But there was a problem. There was no parking space to the right of Ellen's parking place. That meant there would have been no car immediately nearby under which Toby or Amanda could have slipped the Bulldog head without being seen.

Wishbone barked impatiently.

"Just give me a second," Sam said, seeing that the dog had wandered a short distance away.

Then she noticed it. Just in front of Wishbone, a few feet to the right of the parking space, there stood a large trash barrel, the green-plastic type supplied by the town. Yes, it would have been very easy for Toby or Amanda to have secretly slipped the Bulldog head into the trash barrel!

Sam rolled her bike over to the barrel and peered inside. All she saw was ordinary smelly garbage. Nothing in the way of a Bulldog head. But that didn't burn out her theory. Toby or Amanda could have dropped the head in the barrel, then come back for it at a later time. Or someone else could have discovered the head and taken it with them. Or the ill-fated head might now be lying somewhere in the town dump.

Sam briefly considered paying a visit to the town dump. It would have been like Disneyland for Wishbone, Sam thought, but there would be several tons of garbage too many for her taste.

"Okay, let's hit the road," Sam told Wishbone as she swung her bike around. She figured she would make a few more stops before returning to Joe and David.

It was time for a skillful questioning of her two prime suspects—Toby and Amanda.

# Chapter Seven

Wishbone watched a series of small multicolored lights blinking rapidly as they revolved slowly. He and Sam were standing outside the opened door of Toby's bedroom. Sam gave a soft knock at the door.

Toby appeared in the doorway, his hair and clothing looking like they had just been through a tornado. "Uh . . . hi, Sam," he said with confusion. "I'm just working on my project for the Science Club. Well . . . uh . . . would you like to come in?"

"Thanks, don't mind if we do," Wishbone said, as he and Sam entered the room. The blinking lights were part of a bizarre homemade contraption sitting on a table, and Wishbone assumed this was the science project.

"What brings you here?" Toby asked.

"Oh . . ." Sam replied, "I was just riding through the area and figured I'd stop by. Your little sister let me in."

Pretending he was just going about regular dog business, Wishbone took a walk around the room. It was messy, the floor littered with a mixture of cast-off clothing and cables leading to and from a turned-on computer. Wishbone was really searching to see if the Bulldog head might be hidden somewhere amid the rubble.

*Hmm . . .* Wishbone thought. *Don't see it anywhere. But no one said this was going to be easy.*

Wishbone lay on a bare patch of floor, and Sam sat in a chair. Wishbone decided to leave the interrogation to Sam, because she knew Toby better than he did.

"Tell me about your science project," Sam said to Toby.

Toby went eagerly to the contraption on the table. "It's a detailed demonstration of atomic structure," he explained. "You see, I show the interaction between the electrons, protons, and neutrons as they . . ."

As Toby continued talking, Wishbone kept his eyes on the boy. He knew that real-life detectives always considered suspects from two angles—opportunity and motive. Opportunity meant: Was the suspect in the right place at the correct time to have committed the crime? Motive meant: Did the suspect have something to gain by committing the crime? Wishbone and Sam had established opportunity for both Toby and Amanda. Now they had to determine if either one of them had a motive to get rid of the Bulldog head.

". . . then we go deeper inside the nucleus and see all the individual quarks and gluons."

"That's fascinating stuff," Sam remarked. Though she was acting interested, Wishbone could tell that her mind was mostly occupied with the case at hand.

"I'm trying to finish the project today," Toby said,

"but in a few hours I've got to visit with my dad and his new girlfriend."

Sam nodded with understanding. "My parents are divorced, too. Luckily, I get along great with both of them. How about you?"

Toby muttered something, and Sam requested a repeat.

"I do, too," Toby said, a bit louder. "But the back-and-forth business can be a little time-consuming."

Wishbone could tell that Sam was trying to conduct her investigation delicately. She needed to ease Toby into the Bulldog subject without Toby realizing he was under suspicion.

"I don't see how you do it all," Sam said, her eyes admiring the science project. "On top of homework and everyday life, you've got the Science Club and, well, the Bulldog job. That alone takes a lot of time, doesn't it? I mean, not only do you have the football games to attend, but you've got to practice with the cheerleaders and help them organize the pep rallies, right?"

Suddenly Toby knelt on the floor and muttered, "Yeah. Sometimes I wish I'd never met that Bulldog."

Sam realized she had touched a nerve. Very carefully, she probed further. "But you auditioned for the part. I remember. It was at the end of last year. As I recall, no one even auditioned against you."

"Do you remember why that was?" Toby asked.

Sam thought for a moment. "Yes, I do. Your

brother played the part several years back—the year Sequoyah won the regional football championship. Word got around that your brother was the best Bulldog in Sequoyah history, and everyone figured it was only right that you inherit the role."

Toby nodded solemnly, his eyes cast down at the floor. "That's why I got the part. I wasn't right for it then, and I'm not right for it now. And the worst thing of all is that I didn't even *want* the part. It's just that everybody was *expecting* me to take over the role of the Bulldog—the students, the teachers, even my parents."

"You don't like being the Bulldog, do you?" Sam asked quietly.

Toby fidgeted with a nearby cable, his voice growing in certainty. "I don't know why any kid would want to be a school mascot. You've got to jump around for several hours in a hot, sweaty costume, and you can barely see a thing through it, while all around you people are screaming their heads off. Then, by the time you finally recover from the experience, you've got to go through the whole tiring thing again. Do I *like* being the Bulldog? No! This is, without a doubt, the worst occupation in the entire history of mankind!"

Toby was so upset he accidentally jerked the cable from his computer—which instantly killed the blinking lights. Sam remembered how Toby had snapped the rubber band in the car the day before. Her heart went out to the boy, who was in a nearly impossible situation. But as Sam began to understand the cause of his discomfort, she realized a "Toby motive" was rearing its ugly head.

"Sometimes," Toby said, letting the cable slip

from his hand, "I wish that ol' Bulldog would just go take a flying leap."

*Into a trash barrel,* Sam thought. Everything seemed to fit. Toby hated being the Bulldog, but there was too much pressure on him to allow him to quit. So he dumped the head, hoping that act would somehow just make the job disappear. Yes, Sam was suddenly ninety-nine percent certain Toby was the culprit.

"I hope you're proud of yourself!" Wishbone heard Amanda's voice cry out. "I am wounded. Truly wounded. How could you ever suspect, even for a second, that I might be the cause of this catastrophe!"

Wishbone and Sam stood outside the closed door of Amanda's bedroom. They waited a moment. Hearing nothing more, Sam knocked.

"Oh, hi," Amanda said pleasantly as she opened the door. "What a nice surprise, Sam. Come in. You, too, Wishbone."

"Well, if you insist," Wishbone said, as he and Sam stepped into the room.

"I was just riding through the neighborhood and figured I'd stop by," Sam told Amanda. "Your mom let me in. But if you have company—"

"Oh, no," Amanda said, picking up a slim booklet from her desk. "There's no one here. I was just practicing dialogue from a script. On Tuesday I've got an audition . . . well, a call-back, really, for the school's winter play. It's between me and Crystal for the lead, and it's such a juicy character. It'll just kill me if Crystal gets the part.

I'll probably have to put a hex on her, or something. I can't stand it when I don't get the part I want."

Sam chuckled and Wishbone took a casual stroll around the room. It was spotlessly clean, graced with lacy touches on the curtains and furniture. Wishbone paid special attention to the pile of stuffed animals on Amanda's bed.

*No sign of a Bulldog head,* Wishbone thought. *Okay, Sam, time for the second questioning session.*

Sam sat on the floor, and Wishbone lay down beside her. Amanda took a seat at a vanity table that had a lighted mirror attached to it.

"You're an awfully good actress," Sam remarked. "I'll never forget your performance in last year's spring play."

"Why, thank you," Amanda said, with an offhanded gesture. "And let me tell you, that was *really* acting. I'm not anything at all like that character."

"No," Sam said, "as I recall, she was bossy."

Amanda began brushing her mane of black hair. "Any word on that missing Bulldog head?" she asked casually.

"No word," Sam replied.

Wishbone could tell that Sam was taking a low-key approach to this interview. Unlike Toby, Amanda could be counted on to talk about the Bulldog, or any subject, without much prompting.

After a few more moments of brushing, Amanda said, "You know who would have been a really dynamite Bulldog?"

"No. Who?" Sam asked.

"Me," Amanda answered.

"You?" Sam said with amazement. "I thought you preferred the glamorous parts. I can't imagine you wanting to be a Bulldog at football games."

"But that Bulldog is a *star,*" Amanda said, pointing her brush at Sam. "Or at least it could be if the role was played with the proper passion. When we do these school plays, maybe a hundred people come to each performance, and it's all over after a single weekend. But there are usually several hundred people at the football games, and there's a new one every Saturday. The fans don't just applaud politely the way they do at a play—they scream and stomp and cheer. Don't you see? If someone like me was playing the Bulldog, it would practically be like appearing on Broadway!"

Sam found this information most interesting. She pursued the point. "Then why didn't you audition to be the Bulldog?"

Amanda continued her brushing. "Because Toby was a shoo-in, on account of the fact that his brother was such a big hit in the part. Everyone knew Toby would get it. I wasn't about to set myself up for a failure like that. But sometimes I . . ." The brush stopped in mid-stroke.

"What?" Sam asked.

"Oh, never mind," Amanda said, suddenly going to her bed and plopping down.

"No, tell me."

"It's nothing."

"It must be something. All of a sudden you seem kind of stressed."

Amanda gripped a nearby teddy bear. "Okay, here's what I'm thinking. We've had only three football games so far this year, and I don't know if I can make it through the season. It drives me crazy watching Toby butcher that Bulldog role. He's totally wrong for the role, and everyone knows it. In a very nice way, I tried to give him some advice yesterday, but you saw how he bit into me. The truth is, Toby should be impeached. But you can only do that to the President, not a school mascot!"

Amanda glared at the teddy bear. Sam remembered Amanda's irritated expression yesterday, when Toby told her to lay off. Sam sympathized with Amanda, who was also in a nearly impossible situation. But as Sam began to understand the cause of Amanda's frustration, she realized an "Amanda motive" was rearing its ugly head.

"I know I shouldn't say this," Amanda said, tossing the teddy bear aside. "But I really feel someone should just yank the Bulldog job away from Toby."

*And stuff it in a trash barrel,* Sam thought. It made perfect sense. Amanda desired the Bulldog job, but she never had a chance at it. So she figured if she couldn't play the part, she'd dump the head, and no one would play it. Yes, Sam was suddenly ninety-nine percent certain Amanda was the culprit.

Which was a problem. Because Toby and Amanda could not *both* be responsible for the Bulldog's mysterious disappearance. Sam realized she would have to go a step deeper inside the minds of these two suspects.

# Chapter Eight

"**S**o we're leaning toward either Toby or Amanda as the head-snatcher," Wishbone informed David and Joe.

He and Sam were back at the Talbot driveway, where Sam had just brought the boys up to date on the discoveries she and Wishbone had made. Both boys looked dirty, rumpled, and tired. Wishbone noticed an assortment of tools and utensils scattered alongside Ellen's sport utility vehicle.

"We spent almost three hours working on this car," David said, placing tools back in the toolbox. "That locksmith you talked with was right, Sam. There's no way an amateur could have broken into this vehicle without leaving some sign of entry. We've tried hangers, tools, all types of wires, even silverware. No luck. Joe, your mom will be glad to hear this car is a fortress."

"Oh, by the way," Joe said, as he helped David clean up. "We had lunch without you. Sorry, but you were taking a long time, and we didn't know where you were."

"That's okay," Sam said. "I'm not really hungry."

"Hey, *I'm* hungry," Wishbone said, springing up to his hind legs. "Come to think of it, I'm starving. I never did get that brunch, and then I missed lunch. Now I certainly hope you don't expect me to hold out all the way to dinner time. That would be inhuman!"

"I'll help you guys finish cleaning up," Sam said, kneeling on the ground.

Wishbone fell to four feet, sensing that satisfying his appetite was not next on the day's agenda. *I don't believe this. It'll be a good five minutes before they get this place organized. I can't hold out that long. . . . Oh, yeah, I can just fetch a bone from Wanda's yard. . . . Oh, wait— no. . . . I may not be able to reach my bones because of that tunnel-digging trespasser. Oh, well, why don't I give it a try.*

Wishbone trotted toward Wanda's yard. But just before he crossed the driveway that divided the two properties, he stopped dead in his tracks.

The enemy was in view.

In one of the flower beds, there stood a creature. It was some sort of furry animal, roughly the color of a peanut. The size was somewhat bigger than a rat, but somewhat smaller than a cat.

*What, exactly, is it? I need a closer look.*

Wishbone lowered his head, back, and tail to make himself as invisible as possible. Then he crept forward—slowly, silently, eyes focused on the target. Finally, when he was just a bone-toss away from the creature, he stopped.

The animal's body was shaped like a chubby sausage, its fur stiff and bristly. Grasping a flower in its claws, the creature gnawed greedily at the stringy root. Wishbone noticed a very long pair of jutting front teeth.

*Aha! It's a gopher!*

Just then, Wishbone heard the rumble of an approaching car. When the gopher jerked its head around for a look, Wishbone caught a glimpse of two tiny black eyes.

Amazingly fast, the gopher dropped the flower and scampered across the dirt. The next thing Wishbone knew, the gopher seemed to vanish into thin air.

Wishbone ran over to the garden to have a closer look. Once there, he saw no sign of the gopher, except for a small mound of dirt and several flowers that were thrown aside. Then Wishbone saw Wanda pull up in the driveway in her old convertible. Ignoring the car, he began digging through the mound. He figured that was where the gopher's escape hatch was. Wishbone decided he might at least try to issue a warning into the hole.

"Wishbone," Wanda called out after getting out of the car and shutting the door, "you're not bothering those flowers, are you?"

"No, of course not," Wishbone called back.

Wanda tramped over. Soon she was kneeling beside Wishbone. She picked up one of the fallen purple flowers and cried out with grief, "My precious petunias have been mutilated!"

"Look, it wasn't me," Wishbone said, still digging. "It was a gopher."

"I spend one day away from my garden," Wanda said, her voice trembling with emotion, "and look what you go and do!"

Wishbone stopped his digging and turned to Wanda. "I said it was a gopher. G-O-P-H-E-R—you know, those furry little rodents with the really big front teeth."

Wanda held one of the mangled flowers in front of Wishbone's face. "Have you no shame? To take such lovely creations as these in the prime of their life! It is a crime!"

"Wanda," Wishbone said reasonably, "why would I eat those things? True, I keep a diverse diet. I eat meat, cereal, toys, potato chips, occasionally paper and cardboard products, and now and then a leather shoe. *But,* I am not now—nor have I ever been—an eater of flowers!"

Wanda gave a threatening finger wag. "Wishbone, I'm giving you an official warning. If you can't leave my flowers in peace, I will have to remove you permanently from my yard!"

Wishbone turned to face the Talbot house, where he saw his companions now sitting on the front porch. "Hey, Joe, Sam, David!" he called. "Help me out here, guys! Somebody call a lawyer!"

But no one seemed to be listening, and Wanda was already walking angrily toward her front door. Figuring he had better steer clear of Wanda for a while, Wishbone ran back across the driveway and joined the kids on the porch.

"Hi, there," Joe said, stroking the dog's back. "Where ya been, boy?"

"I was being framed by a gopher, thank you," Wishbone said as he sat at Joe's feet. "But don't stop what you're doing. It's calming my nerves very nicely."

"It's getting close to four," David said, checking his watch. "I better get a move on soon. I've got a whole mess of homework."

"Yeah," Sam said, staring into the distance. "I've got homework, too."

Wishbone thought he glimpsed the gopher moving across the yard. But then he realized it was just a tree's shadow lengthening under the fading afternoon sun.

"Hey," Joe said, still petting the dog. "I just thought of something. Is there any way the Bulldog head could have been stolen by those three Jefferson football players we saw at the game yesterday?"

"I don't see how," Sam replied. "There would be no way for them to get inside the car."

"This is a very tough case," David commented.

"True," Sam said. "But, all in all, I'd say we're doing fairly well. Thanks to John Dickson Carr, we've more or less eliminated all possibilities except for Toby and Amanda. You know, I feel badly for both of them, but . . . I'll deal with that after I find the head."

"Well, we better find it soon," David pointed out. "That is, if you want it repaired and back in action by the game at Jefferson next Saturday."

"That's right," Joe said, scratching the underside of Wishbone's neck. "If we can manage to beat Jefferson, that might give us the momentum to have a really great season. But our players are nervous about this game. They need every bit of support they can get—which means it might be nice if the mascot wasn't headless."

Wishbone saw Sam take a deep breath. *I can sense what she's thinking,* he thought. *The stakes are high on this case. And though her friends are being helpful, she thinks the responsibility for finding the Bulldog head is resting mostly on her own two shoulders.*

"Don't you worry," Sam said, resolve in her voice. "One way or another, I am going to find that head and unmask the culprit who stole it."

"That's the spirit!" Wishbone said with admiration. Then he glanced over at Wanda's yard. "And, doggone it, one way or another, I am going to get rid of that darn gopher!"

# Chapter Nine

Tick . . . tick . . . tick . . .

Sam glanced at the round clock on the wall. It was 9:17 on Monday morning, and she was sitting in her eighth-grade Earth Science class. But her mind was on the locked-car mystery, not the current classroom topic, which was dinosaurs. Although neither Toby nor Amanda was in her class, Sam had decided to watch them both closely today, in a search for further clues. Time was running short.

"Sam, which one do you think it was?"

Sam realized that Mrs. Prescott, the gracious white-haired teacher, was talking to her. "I beg your pardon?" Sam asked.

"Which theory do you favor for the extinction of the dinosaurs?" Mrs. Prescott said. "The Ice Age Theory, or the Giant Meteor Theory."

"I'm sorry, but . . . at this point, I'm not really sure."

"Well, don't think you're alone," Mrs. Prescott said in her kindly way. "Many a scientist has thrown up his or her hands in frustration, realizing he or she may never know which of these two theories is true."

*That might be fine for the dinosaurs,* Sam thought, *but it's not good enough for my case. I'm going to find out which of those two kids stole that head—and I'm doing it today.*

At 10:43 Sam sat in American History class, keeping a careful eye on Toby, who sat several desks up and to the right.

"From start to finish, the Boston Tea Party was quite a daring operation." Mr. Levinsky, the enthusiastic teacher who always wore a bow tie, was lecturing. "The preparation, the execution, and even the aftermath were all dangerous. Because, afterward, you see, many of the participants were questioned by authorities about the raid. And these men knew if they showed even a shadow of their guilt, they would be hanged as traitors to the British Crown."

Sam watched Toby stick a finger deep in his mouth, most likely probing for something caught in his braces. Was this boy daring enough to have stolen that head? Sam wondered.

"Now, let's leave the Tea Party," Mr. Levinsky said. "I want everyone to get out your homework assignment." Sam opened her notebook and pulled out several pages stapled together. Over the weekend, the students were supposed to have written a brief biography of a major player in the American Revolution.

"I'd love to hear a few of these out loud," the teacher said, sitting on the edge of his desk. "Let's see . . . who hasn't presented any oral report for a while. How about . . . uh . . . Toby?"

Toby removed the finger from his mouth and muttered something.

"You'll have to speak up, son," Mr. Levinsky said.

Toby spoke louder. "I'm afraid I don't have mine."

Mr. Levinsky turned suddenly serious. "I was very clear that these assignments were due today."

Fear registered on Toby's face, the kind a student got when he knew he had one millisecond to come up with a good excuse for why he hadn't completed the homework assignment.

"I . . . uh . . . well . . ." Toby stammered. "It's rather complicated, but . . . because my mind was . . . well, I was sidetracked by this science . . . then I had to go visit my dad and his . . . and, uh, just before I left, I got a bad case of hiccups, which is true, or . . . no, what I really mean is . . ."

Mr. Levinsky now looked more amused than angry. "You just didn't do it, did you, Toby?"

A few giggles escaped from students throughout the room. "No, sir," Toby admitted. "I guess I just didn't do it."

"Bring it tomorrow," Mr. Levinsky said. "Melanie, what about you?"

Melanie stood and proudly announced, "I have chosen Abigail Adams as my subject."

"Wonderful," the teacher said. "Let's hear it."

As Melanie began reading her biography, Sam kept a close watch on Toby. She was making a significant discovery—*Toby O'Shaughnessy is a terrible actor. That's why he was less than spectacular in the Bulldog role,* Sam thought, *and that's why he made complete mincemeat out of his homework excuse. Bad actors can't play animals, and they certainly can't lie very well.*

This second point was important to the case. The previous day, Sam had sat in Toby's bedroom and carried on a detailed conversation about the Bulldog. *Maybe all the pressure weighing upon Toby could have driven him to steal the Bulldog head, but there's no way he could have fooled anyone* afterward, Sam concluded. *If Toby had been a participant in the Boston Tea Party, he would have been hanged. And if he had stolen the Bulldog head, he would have cracked yesterday afternoon.*

Toby noticed Sam looking at him, and he gave her a small wave. *If Toby had stolen that head,* Sam told herself, *he wouldn't even be able to meet my eyes.* Sam waved back, knowing it was time to cross Toby off the suspect list.

". . . it is my opinion," Melanie said, concluding her report, "that Abigail Adams was one of this country's most fiercely independent women."

At 11:32, Sam sat in Algebra class, casting a sideways glance at Amanda, who sat two desks directly to her left.

Miss Cammack, the teacher who dressed like a drill sergeant, stood by an equation written on the blackboard. "So you see," she said, pointing with her chalk, "if five and three-quarters minus *x* equals three and five-eighths, then *x* simply has to be two and an eighth. There is no other possible answer. Don't let the fractions throw you off. Remember, fractions aren't frustrating, they're fun!"

A few grumbles rumbled around the room.

Miss Cammack picked up a stack of papers and began handing them out briskly. "Now, I'm afraid it's time for that little quiz I warned you about. I have to run down the hall and make copies of some exercises. But I have confidence no one in this room will cheat. And, that those of you who finish early will kindly keep quiet, out of respect for those still working."

With the quiz distributed, the teacher left the room. Miss Cammack was right about no one cheating, but not the keeping-quiet part. A number of students, including Sam, quickly finished the quiz. Then the gossip session began.

Eyes fixed on her desk, Sam tuned in her ears to the loudest gossip station—Amanda. She was already conversing with Betsy, her best friend of the moment.

"I wouldn't tell this to another living soul except you," Amanda whispered, "but I've realized I really do like him. And if I'm going to have a boyfriend this year—and I'm not sure I want one—he would be the best option."

"Does he know this?" Betsy inquired.

"No!" Amanda whispered emphatically. "And you better not tell him—or anyone else, for that matter. If he knows I like him before I know he likes me, then I've lost the upper hand in this relationship."

Sam felt guilty for eavesdropping on this top-secret information, but she was a girl with a mission. Amanda moved speedily through a few other topics.

Then Sam tuned in with all the ear power that she could possibly muster.

". . . even get me started on that Toby O'Shaughnessy," Amanda whispered to Betsy. "He doesn't care any more about that Bulldog job than I care about joining the school Latin Society!"

Sam expected a bombshell any second—a boast from Amanda that she had gotten rid of the head for the sake of her sanity, and perhaps also for the greater good of the school. But Sam was disappointed to hear the gossip immediately shift to the subject of winter play auditions. That was it. No more bulletins on the Bulldog.

As Amanda rambled on about her superior acting talent, Sam realized Amanda Hollings was a big talker. Whatever secrets she had, she expressed them, if not to one person, then to another.

This was important to the case. Amanda may not have confided in Sam about stealing the Bulldog head, but the odds were *overwhelming* that she would have confided in Betsy, her current best friend. And the subject would have come up somehow just a minute ago. It was rather like an algebra equation. If Amanda had stolen the Bulldog head, then: "Secret Confessions to Betsy" plus "Talk of Bulldog" would certainly equal "Confession of Stealing Bulldog Head."

". . . and I'm only telling you this," Amanda whispered to Betsy, "because I trust you with my deepest thoughts, no matter what they are."

Sam let out a sigh, knowing it was time to cross Amanda off the suspect list.

Miss Cammack swept into the room and said, "I trust everyone has easily solved their problems by now!"

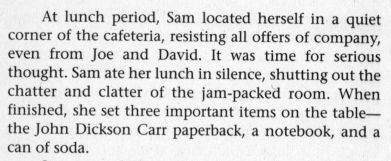

At lunch period, Sam located herself in a quiet corner of the cafeteria, resisting all offers of company, even from Joe and David. It was time for serious thought. Sam ate her lunch in silence, shutting out the chatter and clatter of the jam-packed room. When finished, she set three important items on the table— the John Dickson Carr paperback, a notebook, and a can of soda.

Sam opened *The Hollow Man* to Chapter 17, which was titled "The Locked-Room Lecture." Yesterday she and her friends had determined the only methods that could apply to their locked-car case were Method 5 (Toby), Method 7 (Amanda), and Method 8 (breaking in). But now each of these three methods seemed pretty much out of the question.

Since John Dickson Carr was the master of the

locked-room mystery, logic told Sam it was quite likely the answer would lie in one of Carr's other methods. She spent the next ten minutes carefully reexamining the list. In her notebook she jotted down thoughts, drew diagrams, and crossed things out.

Finally, she determined there was only one other method that had even a slim chance of applying to the locked-car case, and that was Method 2—the one in which the victim was "impelled" to kill himself by either poisonous gas or a ghost. A ghost *could* have slipped into the car and stolen the head—*if,* and this was a gigantic "IF"—there really *was* such a thing as a ghost. Which Sam knew there wasn't. . . .

Or was there? Miss Gilmore seemed to believe in ghosts, and she was an intelligent person. In fact, in the past, Sam had spoken with several other people, all of them reasonable, who claimed to have had an encounter with a ghost. And in *The Hollow Man,* even Dr. Gideon Fell briefly considered the possibility of a ghost in his case. In addition, there *were* rumors about a ghost with a strong loyalty to Jefferson Middle School.

Sam glanced out a window, seeing the bleakness of a gray day. That morning a cold front had blown in, something that usually didn't happen until around Halloween.

Sam knew that a good detective left no stone unturned in the search for the truth. Perhaps she should at least pay a visit to Jefferson and ask some questions there. If she found no real evidence of the ghost, well, then, no harm would have been done.

Sam took a sip of soda and decided that very afternoon she would investigate the existence of the Jefferson Ghost.

A memory oozed into Sam's mind, a scene from a horror movie she and her dad had recently rented. An elderly blind professor with solid white eyeballs leaned toward a young woman and whispered, "My dear, once you begin exploring the spirit world, the spirit world begins exploring you."

# Chapter Ten

Wishbone was beginning to wonder if the gopher had been just a figment of his imagination. He had spent the past few hours in Wanda's yard, waiting patiently behind a shrub for the gopher to reappear. But so far there had been no sign of the furry fellow.

"He *must* be real," Wishbone told himself. Earlier in the day, he had searched for his buried bones. He had found that, indeed, many of them had shifted out of reach, due to a complex network of underground tunnels. He had also found more abandoned flowers in the various flower beds.

A gust of wind blew, causing Wishbone to shiver. Grim clouds sailed through the sky, and a slight wintry chill hung in the air. *Hardly ideal weather for gopher-watching,* Wishbone thought. *I'd be much happier curled up on my big red chair in Ellen's study.*

At that moment, Wanda stepped out her front door, wearing a coat and a cap with funny-looking earflaps. She walked to her car, seemed to remember something, then walked over to one of the gardens.

"Oh, no!" she gasped, picking up a handful of

destroyed flowers. Then she scurried over to another garden, bent down, and then picked up more dead flowers, and cried out, "This is murder! Murder most foul! All my flowers are being massacred!"

She stood up, turned, scanned the yard, then fixed her eyes in Wishbone's direction.

"Wishbone!" she cried in a shrill voice. "I see you there behind that shrub. Come out at once!"

"Give me a break," Wishbone pleaded. "I'm on a stake-out here!"

"Wishbone!" Wanda yelled.

"Well, now my cover's blown for sure," Wishbone grumbled, as he stepped out from behind the shrub.

Wanda marched up to Wishbone and said angrily, "I gave you fair warning about those flowers. Yet you have continued to carry on with your mission of destruction!"

"Hey! Whatever happened to the old saying 'A dog is innocent until proven guilty'?"

Wanda stretched her arm, pointing a finger. "Wishbone, when I get back from the beauty parlor, I don't want to see you here. Is that understood? I henceforth banish you from my yard!"

With that, Wanda stomped over to her car, got inside, and slammed the door shut. Wishbone winced at the sharp sound. He actually felt a prick of pain somewhere deep inside. He didn't like being yelled at by anyone, especially when it was a false accusation. Perhaps worst of all, however, was the fact that he was banished from Wanda's yard, his own personal Savings-and-Bone Bank.

Wanda's convertible roared to life. She shot the

car into Reverse and rocketed out of the driveway. With a sinking heart, Wishbone watched the car drive down the street.

Wishbone walked away sadly. Suddenly, his eye caught a streak of peanut-colored motion. He turned and saw that it was the gopher speeding across one of Wanda's gardens. The gopher skidded to a stop, yanked up a flower, then began gnawing greedily at the root.

*He must have popped out of a tunnel the second Wanda hit the street,* Wishbone thought. *Isn't he a sneaky one! Well, this toothy intruder has caused a lot of trouble around here, and it's time I take action. I'm going to have a little talk with him, man-to-man—or, rather, dog-to-rodent. Yes, sir, it's time to lay down the ground rules of this yard.*

With supreme confidence, Wishbone trotted right over to the gopher and said, "Excuse me, sir. Yes, young man, I am speaking to *you.*"

The gopher continued to chow down on the flower without so much as a glance at Wishbone.

"All right," Wishbone said, "so maybe you don't understand English. I know most animals don't. But you *will* understand the ways of nature."

At once, Wishbone assumed the classic canine position for a standoff—ears erect, tail high, fur bristling. Summoning all his canine power, he gave a low-throated threatening growl.

Very slowly, the gopher turned to face Wishbone, his mouth muscles still munching away. He looked the dog up and down with his beady black eyes, as if to say, "Who do you think you are, pal, and why are you bothering me?"

Wishbone peeled back his lips, showing his glistening teeth in all their menacing glory.

The gopher tossed his half-chewed flower at Wishbone's paws. Then he yanked up another flower and began to devour its root with gusto.

Wishbone unleashed a loud bark. The sound rang throughout the yard like a clap of thunder.

The gopher looked at Wishbone, showing his prominent pair of front teeth. His chubby stub of a body began to jiggle. Wishbone was not sure, but he somehow got the feeling the gopher was laughing at him.

# Chapter Eleven

Sam listened to Joe and David make wisecracks as the three of them steered their bikes along a winding road.

"This is just how I wanted to spend the rest of my afternoon," Joe called out. "Ghost-hunting!"

"It's a great after-school activity," David called back. "Whoops! I forgot my ghost-meter!"

"I'm not saying there really *is* a ghost," Sam remarked with some annoyance. "I just think we should look into the possibility. Is that asking so much? If I'm not mistaken, I've helped both of you with stunts a lot crazier than this!"

Right after school had let out that day, Sam had convinced Joe and David to ride over to Jefferson Middle School with her. They started making jokes immediately.

"You know, Sam," David said, "I hate to say it, but I think this case is driving you out of your head!"

Both boys howled with laughter at that remark.

"Maybe you guys are just afraid of the ghost," Sam said in a teasing tone.

Joe and David's laughter died down, and Sam wondered if her last statement might just have been true. She had grown a little nervous about looking for this ghost herself. The chilly wind whipped around Sam as she gripped her handlebar. She was glad she had worn her heavier jacket today. Before long, the trio arrived at Jefferson. They parked and locked their bikes, then went to one of the school's side doors. Finding it open, they entered.

This section of the school seemed empty, and every footstep they took in the hall echoed off the walls of lockers. It was always weird being in school after hours, Sam thought, but it felt especially weird in someone else's school.

"What do we say if a teacher stops us?" David asked.

"We tell whoever it is that we're looking for the eighth-grade Supernatural Class," Joe joked.

"We'll just tell the teacher exactly why we're here," Sam said. "We're not trying to break any rules. We just want some information. Maybe you guys better let me do all the talking." The truth was, Sam wasn't really sure how to go about investigating the ghost. She just planned to play things by ear.

Sam and her friends came to another hallway. To the left, Sam heard students' voices in a room; to the right, she heard a steady swishing sound.

"This way," Sam said, leading Joe and David to the right.

Sam followed the vaporous odor of ammonia to a classroom, then looked inside. All the desks were shoved to the sides, and a custodian was busy mopping the floor. His gray hair was roughly the same shade as his uniform, and he had a narrow, hawklike nose. The name "Mickey" was stitched over his shirt pocket.

"Excuse me," Sam said to Mickey, "but I have a really dumb question."

"That's what schools are for," Mickey remarked. He had a dry delivery, but Sam could tell there was humor beneath it.

Sam, Joe, and David entered the room, but they stayed near the door. Sam figured she would come right out with her question. "Have you ever heard of the Jefferson Ghost?"

Mickey finished mopping a patch of floor, then said, "That's not a dumb question."

"So you've heard of it?" Joe asked.

"Not just heard *of* it," Mickey said in a perfectly natural manner. "I've heard *it*. Seen it, too . . . sort of."

"Oh, come on," David said. "You're kidding us."

Mickey gave David a sly glance. Then he plunged his mop into a bucket and swirled it around. "Believe me, I'm not the only one. Over the years, a lot of folks claim they've seen evidence of that ghost, especially at Jefferson games—you know, helping out the team. Once, at basketball game, a Jefferson shot bounced off the backboard, hit the floor, then bounced straight up into the basket for a score. Myself, I'm a sports fan, but I've never seen that before."

"It's strange," Joe said, "but it could happen."

"As you may or may not know," Mickey continued, "so far Jefferson has won all of its football games this year by huge leads. They beat a team last week by forty-five points. Well, a lot of people, including myself,

think Mr. Winslow might be partly responsible. I mean, the team's good this year, but, come on, I've seen them play—they're not *that* good!"

Sam could not tell whether Mickey was joking or not. "Is Mr. Winslow the ghost?" Sam asked.

"That's right," Mickey said, squeezing the mop dry. "Before he was a ghost, he was a biology teacher here. Real nice fellow, Simon Winslow. I remember him well. Loved this school like it was his family home. Went to every play, game, ceremony—you name it. But eleven years ago he was killed in a car crash. Tragic thing. Shortly after that, people began to suspect he was haunting some of the sporting events."

"Have you seen or heard this ghost anywhere else besides at the games?" David inquired.

Mickey pulled the mop out of the pail, then leaned on the long handle. "Room two-oh-six. The Biology laboratory. In my opinion, that's where he hangs out most of the time. He doesn't bother the classes, no, sir. But soon after Mr. Winslow's death, I began hearing a rattling in the closet most every day I was alone in there cleaning. Now and then, the lights flickered, too—even though there was nothing wrong with them. And once or twice, sure as I'm standing here, I swear I heard Mr. Winslow's voice floating in the air."

Sam studied the man's wrinkled face. She now felt fairly certain he was playing it straight with her and her friends. "Do you think the ghost might be in there now?" she asked.

"Most likely," Mickey replied.

"Could we have a look?" Sam said.

A ghost of a smile crept across the custodian's lips. "If that's what you kids want . . ."

Sam, Joe, and David followed Mickey down an empty hallway, up a flight of steps, then along another deserted hallway. It took a while to make the trek, because Mickey had a limp. But finally the group stopped in front of Room 206. With some jangling, Mickey singled out a key on his giant key ring and turned it in the lock cylinder. Then he opened the door.

"We keep all the rooms locked after school lets out," Mickey said, his hand on the doorknob. "Come find me downstairs when you're done. Me, I don't go in this room much anymore. I like to let the guy rest in peace."

Sam felt a wave of weirdness wash over her. The man really seemed to believe a ghost lived inside the laboratory. "Okay," she told Mickey. "Thanks."

Sam entered the room, with Joe and David following. The window shades were half drawn, leaving only a blurry dimness in the place. Long tables with chairs surrounded a large counter with work space and two stainless-steel sinks. A collection of glass jars sat on the counter. In each jar, a dead object floated in a clear sea of formaldehyde. Sam noticed frogs, mice, and birds.

"I guess they're dissecting now," David said, nodding at the jars.

The previous year, Sam had dissected an animal for the first time. Though unsettled by the experience, she also found it fascinating. From one of the jars, Sam caught sight of a frog's yellow eye. "Turn on the lights," she told Joe.

Joe flipped up three light switches. The overhead fluorescent lights flickered, then died out. Joe worked the switches up and down a few times, but the lights refused to come on.

"Why did that happen?" Sam asked David.

"Uh . . . well . . ." David said, looking up. "There could be an electrical problem." David was one of the most scientific-minded people Sam knew. But at the moment, he seemed hesitant, maybe even scared.

Joe may have also been scared, but he seemed determined not to show it. "There *has* to be an electrical problem," he stated firmly. "Because there's not a ghost in here. Got it? No ghost. It's impossible!"

Something crashed, causing a loud metallic clang.

Everyone froze. This was followed by a hollow knocking sound, like a horse's hooves clattering on pavement.

Sam felt a queasy feeling rise up from her stomach and move through her chest until it clutched at her throat. She realized this feeling was Pure Terror. In a raspy voice, she managed to say, "What was that?"

"I think it came from the closet over there," David said, not moving a muscle.

Joe blew his hair upward with an irritated huff. He made his way to the closet, then tried turning and pulling the knob. But the door would not open. "It's locked," he said. "Help me find something to pry it open with."

Joe and David began looking around the room, searching the tabletops and looking inside drawers. Almost against her will, Sam's eyes drifted to the collection of jars—the flightless birds, the tiny white mice, the sideways frog. Sam found herself focusing on the frog's round belly. As she stared at it, she became aware that the frog moved slightly in the fluid. In the hazy half-light, the creature seemed at least partially alive. Maybe there was a state of being somewhere between life and death, Sam thought.

Then Sam realized she was hearing an unfamiliar voice.

". . . don't see anything to use to open the door," David was saying.

"Shh!" Sam interrupted.

"What is it?" Joe asked.

"Listen," Sam whispered.

Everyone fell silent. In a tone low and eerie, the voice was singing a solemn melody:

> "Oh, Jefferson is my alma mater
> And so always a part of me,
> And though my stay here may be brief,
> Forever do I pledge my faith to thee."

# Chapter Twelve

After one verse, the song faded into silence.

For a long moment no one moved or spoke. By then, even Joe was noticeably spooked.

"That song must be the Jefferson alma mater," David finally uttered.

"I think it was coming from the closet," Joe murmured.

Sam took a slow breath, then said, "I want to do one of two things—either prove that wasn't a ghost, or get out of here immediately."

"Hold on a sec," Joe said, seeming to get an idea.

He rushed out of the room, and a moment later Sam heard a knock inside the closet.

Joe returned and said, "Did you hear that knock?"

Sam and David nodded. "A lot of these classroom closets are shared by two rooms," Joe explained. "I went to the room next door and went inside the closet. Since you heard my knock, that means it was the same closet. There was no one there, but I saw some supplies and junk that could have been used to cause those noises, and anybody could have been in there singing—if they were good with locks, or if they had the right keys."

"David, check the lights," Sam instructed.

Using a chair, David stepped up onto one of the tables. Then he pulled a plastic covering off one of the fluorescent light fixtures and handed it to Joe. He fiddled with a fluorescent tube. The light flickered, then beamed brightly.

"The light tube was just twisted out of place," David called down. "It's easy to do. Someone could have done all of them in less than a minute."

Sam realized that David was back to his old scientific self. "So you don't think that was a ghost?" she asked with relief.

"No," David said, returning the light cover to its place. "Twisting a light tube is definitely a human thing."

"In other words," Joe observed, "somebody was having some fun with us. But who?"

"Maybe Mickey," David said, jumping down from the table. "Sounds in the closet, trouble with the lights, a floating voice. Those are all things he claimed he heard or saw from Mr. Winslow's ghost. And let's not forget—he's got keys for everything."

"I don't know," Sam said doubtfully. "Why wouldn't he relock that room next door? And why would he have fiddled with the lights *before* he knew someone would come around asking about the ghost?"

"Hmm . . ." David said, "good questions."

"Okay. Let's go tell Mickey we're done," Joe advised. "We'll just thank him and say nothing at all happened. If he is the practical joker, there's no point in giving him any satisfaction by letting him know we were spooked."

Joe and David left the room, but Sam stayed a moment to cast a last glance at the creatures in the glass jars. Despite her relief, she realized that she was a little disappointed she had not met a visitor from the afterlife. "Good-bye, everyone," she whispered before leaving.

Mickey showed no sign of deviousness when Sam and her friends went back to him. When Mickey asked whether or not they had seen the ghost, they simply said no and thanked him for his help. Then they left the building.

As the trio unlocked their bikes, David said, "I have to admit, I got some serious creeps in that room. But I still think most of the ghosts people believe they see are a result of pranks, or their imagination running wild. And that includes the Jefferson Ghost."

"I agree," Joe said. "What do you think, Sam?"

Sam zipped up her jacket. "When I was in that Biology lab, I got a funny feeling that the Jefferson Ghost really *could* exist. But if he does exist, I'd like to think he would have some dignity. In other words, I don't think he would go around scaring kids or breaking into cars. I'm crossing Mr. Winslow off the suspect list. Exactly who was in the closet—well, that's another question."

When the trio arrived back in their own neighborhood, Joe and David peeled off to run some errands for David's mom. They invited Sam to go along, but she chose to keep on biking over to Pepper Pete's.

The restaurant was almost empty, except for an elderly couple and a mother with a small child.

"Hi," another waitress greeted Sam when she entered. "If you're looking for your dad, he's not here. He went to pick up some supplies, but he should be back in about an hour."

"Okay," Sam said. "I'm just going to hang out for a few minutes."

Sam took a seat and set her knapsack down on the table. The truth was, she *had* gone to the pizza parlor specifically to see her dad. She was feeling at the end of her rope with the case of the missing mascot head. She figured her dad might have some advice, or at least a comforting word. Sam had thought of calling her mom, but then she remembered she was halfway across the country at the moment.

Sam glanced across the room at the small child, who was trying to unzip his mother's purse. "No!" the mother scolded. "You're not supposed to go in there, sweetheart."

Sam felt her hopes leap up. *Of course!* she thought. *The answer is clobbering me over the head!* On Saturday someone could have secretly taken Mrs. Talbot's purse, fished out her car key, and used it to get inside the car and snatch the Bulldog head. Then he or she could have put the key and purse back without anyone noticing it was ever missing. That would be a variation on Method 8, breaking in. The restaurant had been busy that evening, and someone could possibly have picked up the purse without Ellen, Sam, or anyone else at the table witnessing it.

Sam rushed to the restaurant's pay phone and quickly looked up the number for the Oakdale Public Library in the phone book. Then she inserted a quarter, dialed, held her breath a moment. A ring, another ring, another . . .

"Library," a female voice answered.

"Mrs. Talbot," Sam said, recognizing the voice, "it's me, Sam."

"Hi," Ellen said cheerfully.

"A thought just occurred to me," Sam said, all business. "While you were in Pepper Pete's on Saturday, is it possible someone took your purse, borrowed your car key, then returned the key and purse without you knowing it?"

"I'm afraid it's not possible," Ellen replied. "I always keep my car key in my pocket when I wear pants, which I was on Saturday. You had a good idea, though."

Sam felt her hopes crashing to the ground. After a heavy sigh, she said, "Well, thanks. I'm sorry to have bothered you."

"Sam, are you all right? You sound a little upset."

"I guess I am upset."

"About that missing Bulldog head?"

"Yes," Sam said, suddenly feeling overpowered by her emotions. "As it is, it's going to be very difficult for us to beat Jefferson on Saturday. And if I don't find that head, the Sequoyah Bulldogs are going to be without a *Bulldog!* I've analyzed all of John Dickson Carr's methods, and I've racked my brain for three days straight, but I still can't make heads or tails out of this case. You told me there would be a logical explanation, but there isn't, Mrs. Talbot. There just isn't!"

Ellen spoke in a gentle tone. "Sam, you're doing your absolute best. And, no matter what happens, we'll all be extremely proud of you. You know that, don't you?"

"I guess so," Sam said with a faint smile.

After a few more minutes of conversation, Sam hung up the phone and returned to her seat. Thanks to Mrs. Talbot, she was feeling somewhat better—even though she was still no closer to the very necessary task of finding the missing mascot head.

Sam unzipped her knapsack and pulled out the paperback copy of *The Hollow Man*. She gazed at the black silhouette of a person that stared out from the cover. The silhouette almost seemed to be teasing her, telling her she would never in a million years discover the identity of the devious head-thief.

"H'mf ha," Sam uttered, in imitation of Dr. Gideon Fell.

At once, Sam realized yet another reason why she had to solve the case—simply because she *wanted* to. For the most part, she was finding a great deal of satisfaction in playing the role of detective. And in a good mystery story, the detective almost always figured everything out—even if the case seemed impossible.

# Chapter Thirteen

*H'mf, ha,* Wishbone thought. *This situation is looking impossible to fix.* He lay in the front yard of the Talbot house, his front paws folded under his head. Across the driveway, he watched the gopher as it devoured yet another flower in Wanda's yard.

Wishbone called out, "Are you enjoying yourself, my gourmet-loving friend?"

The sky remained an unpleasant gray. A withered leaf drifted to the ground, then blew mournfully by.

*There must be some solution, though. Something, somehow. If I don't clear my name in the very near future, word will spread from door to door that I'm a "flower-eater." I'll be blacklisted from every yard in the neighborhood!*

Wishbone heard an unpleasant sound coming from Wanda's house. At first he thought it was an out-of-tune accordion, but then he realized it was Wanda singing in the kitchen.

*The gopher's out here feasting on her flowers, and she doesn't even notice. Maybe she doesn't even care. Maybe she's busy whipping up a flower soufflé for him to take home to his tunnel.*

Wishbone lifted his head. A thought arrived.

*Wanda still doesn't* know *about the gopher!* Wishbone realized. *That's the problem. She's always going when the gopher's coming, or coming when the gopher's going. But right now, even as I lay here moping, Wanda and the gopher are both around at the exact same moment in time! It's a long shot, but maybe, just maybe, I can arrange things so . . .*

Almost as fast as a speeding bullet, Wishbone darted across the driveway, into Wanda's yard, past the gopher, and straight to Wanda's front porch. He scratched at the door over and over again. Soon Wanda came from the kitchen and opened the door. She was wearing an apron decorated with embroidered "smiley faces."

"Wishbone," Wanda said, trying to adopt a stern expression, "I told you to stay out of my yard—and I meant it."

"Oh, Wanda," Wishbone said, "you know I have nothing but the utmost respect for everything you say, but if you'll just take a look over at that—"

"I've tried to be reasonable," Wanda continued, "but you've refused to abide by my rules!"

"If you won't listen to me," Wishbone practically shouted, "I'll show you what I'm talking about!"

Wishbone trotted across the yard, stopping right beside the gopher. The gopher paused from his gnawing just long enough to give Wishbone a self-satisfied grin.

Wishbone glanced back at Wanda's front door, but she had already gone back inside. *What's her problem?* Wishbone thought with exasperation. *All she has to do to catch this rascal red-handed is—*

The next thing Wishbone knew, Wanda was charging across the yard, waving a broomstick over her head and screaming like a banshee.

"Get out of my garden, you gluttonous overgrown gopher!!!"

Almost before Wishbone could finish a blink, the gopher disappeared into the ground.

Wanda stood in the yard, staring at the spot where the gopher had been, still waving the broom over her head. "That *wasn't* Wishbone destroying my flowers!" she exclaimed to no one in particular. "It was a gopher!"

"I'm glad you finally see things my way," Wishbone said.

"Oh, Wishbone," Wanda said, suddenly walking over to him and kneeling down to scratch his neck. "I am so sorry. Please accept my heartfelt apology."

"Apology accepted," Wishbone replied. "Could you scratch a little lower, please?"

"And I know just what to do!" Wanda announced.

"Oh, I don't expect too much in the way of your making things up to me," Wishbone said. "Nothing extravagant. In fact, I'd settle for a full-year supply of Prime Grade-A T-bone steaks."

"As soon as I go inside," Wanda thought aloud, "I will get on the telephone and find out where I can purchase some snakes."

"Not *snakes*," Wishbone pointed out. *"Steaks!"*

"Gopher snakes," Wanda continued. "I was just reading about them in *The Horticultural Review*. They say gopher snakes are the best thing in the world to use to drive gophers out of your garden. But first, I'd better stand guard for a while to show that little varmint I mean serious business."

Wanda got up and began to march back and forth, cradling the broom in her arm as if it were a rifle. Wishbone sat in the grass, hoping for a front-row seat in the event of a sudden gopher ambush.

*Hmm . . . gopher snakes,* Wishbone thought. *That sounds like an excellent idea. I suppose they're a breed of snake that make their living terrorizing gophers. A noble occupation, indeed.*

Just then, Wishbone saw Sam pedaling down the street on her bicycle. She pulled into Wanda's driveway, looking at Wanda with a perplexed expression.

Wishbone ran over to her, calling, "Hey, Sam, how's it going? Joe and David aren't around, if that's why you're in the neighborhood. But you might get a chance to see the match of the century—Wild Wanda against the Gluttonous Gopher!"

"Miss Gilmore," Sam called out, "what on earth are you doing?"

Wanda continued to parade back and forth as she spoke. "I discovered a gopher in my garden, and I'm making sure he doesn't come back! Then, when I'm done here, I am going to find out where I can purchase a supply of gopher snakes. I've read they're the best possible defense against a gopher attack."

"Gopher snakes?" Sam said, wrinkling her nose. "Never heard of them."

"Neither have I," Wishbone said, "but I greatly look forward to their arrival."

"Do you know if Joe or David is around?" Sam asked Wanda.

"I haven't seen either one of them," Wanda replied. "But I just came outside."

*Didn't I already tell her they're not around?* Wishbone thought. *Nobody ever listens to the dog.*

"Did you ever solve that mystery about the missing Bulldog head?" Wanda asked.

"No. The search continues," Sam answered. "But you'll be happy to know that I did investigate the Jefferson Ghost. I discovered some interesting information, but I don't think the ghost is the one who stole the head."

"Probably not," Wanda said, shifting the broom to her other hand. "I get a little carried away with my supernatural theories. I guess it's pretty silly to think a ghost would break into a car and steal a mascot head. Sorry if I misled you. Come to think of it, what I'm doing right now is also pretty strange."

Wanda stopped marching and looked at the broom.

"You look strange?" Wishbone told Wanda. "Never."

"Sam, I'll see you later," Wanda said, heading for her house. "Time to find myself some gopher snakes in the phone book!"

Sam chuckled as Wanda disappeared inside. Wishbone placed his front legs against Sam, who was still on her bike. "Now that I've solved my impossible gopher problem," Wishbone said, "what do you say we sit down together, maybe you pet me a little, and I'll help you solve your impossible Bulldog problem?"

Seeing that Wishbone wanted some attention, Sam climbed off her bike and removed her helmet. She sat in the grass of Wanda's yard as Wishbone lay right beside her. "I know what you're after," Sam said, running her hand along the dog's spine.

Wishbone closed his eyes with contentment.

*Snakes,* Sam thought. *Didn't John Dickson Carr mention snakes as a possibility for one of his methods? Yes. He suggested snakes as a possibility for Method 3.* "Murder by a mechanical device already planted in the room," Sam mused out loud. "Boy, by now, I practically know Gideon Fell's locked room lecture by heart. Dr. Fell said a poisonous snake could be planted in a locked room instead of in a mechanical device. Eventually, the snake would slither out of its hiding place and kill the victim. That's of no help to my case, of course, but it's interesting."

Sam reached behind Wishbone's left ear and found his favorite spot to be scratched. The dog's tail thumped with happiness.

As Sam felt the cool breeze blow by, she wondered what her next move should be. Then—very slyly and slowly, a vision slid into Sam's mind. A vision of the eight lock-picking devices she had seen on the counter at the locksmith shop. As if they were lying before her, she saw them gleaming like so many silver snakes.

"Someone must have used those devices to break into the car," Sam said softly. The words came out of her mouth almost before she realized it.

Wishbone half-opened his eyes. Sam continued talking, even though she knew Wishbone couldn't understand her. It helped to give voice to her thoughts.

"Why?" Sam said. "Well, after going through all of John Dickson Carr's methods, I'm getting nowhere with Toby and Amanda. I may have to go back to Method Eight, breaking into the car."

Wishbone opened his eyes a little wider.

Sam continued. "And I've also discovered that the only possible way someone could have broken into the car without leaving a sign of entry is by using those special lock-picking tools."

Wishbone tilted his head, as if curious to hear more.

"The problem is this: Mr. Rosenbaum said those tools could only be purchased by a professional lock-smith—which means the break-in couldn't have been done by an amateur. And he also said a professional locksmith wouldn't let just anybody into a car without seeing proof of ownership—which means the break-in couldn't have been done by a professional. So we're stuck with nothing. Unless . . . I wonder if the culprit could be somebody halfway *between* a professional and an amateur."

Wishbone opened his eyes all the way.

"After all, sometimes I'm a waitress at Pepper Pete's, but I don't really consider myself a regular waitress. I'm just doing it to help my—"

Sam stopped scratching. The dog's ears raised.

"Didn't Mr. Rosenbaum mention that he had a son who sometimes helped him? Yes. He said his son had watched the shop for a little while on Saturday while he was out. I just assumed the son was also a professional locksmith. Maybe he only helps out occasionally, the way I help at Pepper Pete's."

Wishbone got up on all fours, his brown eyes glowing.

"It makes sense, doesn't it, Wishbone? I don't know why the son would want to steal the Bulldog head, but if he's just a kid, well . . . Yes, the son just might be the key to unlocking the locked-car mystery! Come on, Wishbone!"

Sam leaped up, ran to her bike, and quickly strapped on her helmet. After swinging the bike around, she rode out of the driveway and began to pedal down the street. Sam felt her heart spin excitedly with every rotation of the tires. She felt like a first-class detective who had just come up with a brilliant deduction.

Sam noticed Wishbone galloping right alongside her. "I couldn't have done it without you," she called to him. "Now, let's pick up some speed! We've got ourselves a mystery to finish solving!"

# Chapter Fourteen

Sam heard the bell at the door jingle as she and Wishbone stepped inside the locksmith shop of Rosenbaum & Son. Mr. Rosenbaum was alone. He was in the process of taking some packages out of a box and hanging them on the display wall.

Recognizing Sam, he gave her a nod. "How's the mystery business, kiddo?" he asked in his tough, gangster voice. "Did you and your dog ever figure out who busted into that car and made off with the goods?"

"Well, maybe," Sam said with a smile.

"But you need some more expert advice."

Sam took out a key ring from her jacket pocket and pulled off her house key. "Actually, right now I just need a duplicate key made."

Mr. Rosenbaum took the key. "Just one copy?"

"Yes, please." Sam didn't really need a copy of the key. Her request was just a way to hide the real purpose of her visit, which was to get some information about Mr. Rosenbaum's son.

The locksmith attached the key to a small metal machine that sat on the counter. From the wall he pulled a brand-new gold-colored key, which he also attached to the machine, then flipped a switch. As the machine gave a loud mechanical whine, Mr. Rosenbaum slid a mechanism from right to left. Sam could see the machine was somehow cutting an imitation of the grooves of the original key on to the new key. Soon Mr. Rosenbaum shut off the machine and removed both keys, handing Sam the original.

"You certainly know what you're doing," Sam remarked.

"I've been in the locksmithing business a long time," Mr. Rosenbaum said, as he smoothed out the grooves of the new key with a file.

"Does the name 'Rosenbaum and Son' refer to you and your own son?" Sam asked casually.

Mr. Rosenbaum set the new key on the counter and picked up a hammer. "Oh, no. The name actually refers to me and my father. He started this place many years ago, and we worked here together for a while. He's also the one who got me interested in all those old gangster movies. My own son's not a locksmith. He's still in school."

"Oh, really? What school does he go to?"

The key clinked as Mr. Rosenbaum tapped it with the hammer. "Jefferson Middle School."

Sam felt an excited buzz run through her body. "I see. So, in age, your son's just around . . ."

"Fourteen years old," the locksmith said, running a finger over the key. "He just helps out when he's free and feels like it. He's tied up with school activities a lot. He's the . . . uh . . . whatchamacallit . . . the school mascot."

Again the hammer clinked against the key. Sam felt a buzz so strong that she almost jumped.

Mr. Rosenbaum set the glinting gold key on the counter. "There you go. A perfect key. That'll be one dollar."

"Has your son inherited your talent with the tools?" Sam inquired, as she handed over a dollar bill.

"Yeah. He's a chip off the old block," Mr. Rosenbaum said proudly. "In fact, he's almost getting even handier with the tools than I am. He's a regular locksmithing whiz."

Sam felt dizzy with excitement. Inside her mind, everything about the mystery was coming to a head. She now felt one hundred percent certain that the son was the culprit. Not only did he attend Jefferson, but he was the school's mascot. Both of those facts would give him a strong motive for stealing the head. And not only did he have a way to get to the locksmithing tools, but he had the skill to use them properly.

Sam noticed Wishbone looking up at her. "I'm almost done," she told the dog.

Sam tapped her fingers on the counter, wondering what to do next. *Find the son,* she told herself. Looking at her watch, she saw it was almost six o'clock. *Where might he be right now? Home, possibly. And where would he have stashed the head? Also at home, possibly. Okay. Where, exactly, is his home?*

Sam glanced at a framed certificate on the wall. It was a locksmithing document made out to a Mervyn Rosenbaum.

Sam cleared her throat. "Uh . . . do you have a phone book I could borrow?"

"Sure," Mr. Rosenbaum said. He pulled out a phone book from a shelf behind him, and he set it on the counter. With trembling hands, Sam leafed through the book, careful not to let the locksmith see where she was really looking. Rayburn, Roberts, Rollins—Rosenbaum. Mervyn Rosenbaum, 3234 Blackberry Lane. Sam closed the book.

"Well, thanks for everything," Sam told Mr. Rosenbaum. "I hope to see you again sometime."

In his gangster voice, Mr. Rosenbaum replied, "Till we meet again, kiddo."

Wishbone heard the bell jingle as he followed Sam out of the shop. As Sam unlocked her bike, Wishbone said, "I think I followed most of that pretty well. You figured out the son was, indeed, the head-snatcher. Also, if I'm not mistaken, you just looked up his address. Great work, Sam! Really, I mean it. You're turning into quite the detective."

"One more stop," Sam told Wishbone, as she climbed aboard her bike. "The house of Mr. Rosenbaum and his son."

Wishbone flew on all fours as Sam pedaled at a furious pace. After traveling along several unfamiliar streets, they turned on to a block lined with homes. Sam parked in front of a pleasant-looking one-story house, and Wishbone followed her up to the front porch. Sam rang the doorbell.

A moment passed. There was no answer. Sam tapped her foot nervously. Wishbone felt a bit nervous himself, considering how near they might be to the villain of their mystery. Trying to act casual, he lifted his back leg and gave his side a scratch.

*What was that?*

He thought he saw a small movement at one of the windows. Wanting a better look, he slowly turned his head. Sure enough, he noticed the curtain at the window was peeled back just a teeny bit. He could make out the shadowy outline of a human shape behind the curtain.

"Sam," Wishbone whispered, "look, someone's watching us from the window. Sam, can you hear me? Sam?"

Sam didn't seem to get the idea.

*Okay,* Wishbone thought quickly, *if that person at the window is the thief, he might somehow know we're here looking for the head, in which case he probably won't open the door. And even if he does open the door, he probably won't admit to having stolen the head. That means we probably won't get the head back today. But then maybe the head is hidden somewhere on these premises. Let's see . . . When I get hold of something I don't want anyone else to have, what do I do with it? . . . Of course! I bury it!*

"Wait here," Wishbone told Sam. "You'll be the decoy."

Pretending everything was just fine, Wishbone climbed down the porch steps and scanned the front yard with his keen eyes. *Nah! Humans don't usually bury stuff in the ground. They bury it . . .*

Wishbone saw that the garage door was wide open. He slowly walked over, soon stepping inside the dim depths of the garage. A damp, cool, oily smell filled his nostrils, but there was nothing in the scent that gave away the location of the Bulldog head—if, in fact, it *was* there. Wishbone spotted all sorts of other things—tools, sporting equipment, garden supplies, a carton of soda cans, several bikes.

Wishbone strolled up to a coil of green hose and peered over it. Nothing. He stuck his head behind the carton of soda cans. Nothing. At the far end of the garage, he noticed a random pile of cardboard boxes.

*That's a perfect place to bury a head. But I'd better conduct this search really fast. Any second, that shadowy shape behind the window might catch me in the act. Oh, boy, this is a little more danger than I had bargained for. . . . Oh, I should just stop worrying and get to work.*

Wishbone hurried over to the boxes and tried to nudge one of the lower ones out of the way. It was too heavy. Wishbone stepped back to survey the scene. He noticed an oblong bag filled with golf clubs leaning at a low angle against a wall. It was right next to the pile of boxes.

He touched a paw against the golf bag. It seemed steady enough. Very carefully, Wishbone climbed up the leaning bag until he was on a level with the highest box. He could see that particular box was empty. Reaching over as far as he could, Wishbone grabbed a flap of the box in his mouth.

His paws began sliding down the bag's leather surface. He dug in his nails to keep from tumbling off. After getting a better grip on the bag, he eased the top box out of the way. There was now an open space behind several of the lower boxes.

Wishbone looked down—and saw the big brown Bulldog head staring up at him. There it was, sad-looking as ever—drooping ears, missing teeth, sagging eye. *Definitely* the Sequoyah Bulldog!

*Hip-hip-hooray for me! I found the head!*

Something scraped against the wall, and Wishbone realized the golf bag was slipping beneath his weight. He jumped off quickly, and then—*crash!* The case and all of its rattling clubs slammed onto the concrete floor with a tremendous racket.

*Oh, no! What should I do now? I'll be caught for sure. I can't just abandon this head, but . . . I don't know how I can possibly—*

"Wishbone, what are you doing in here?" Sam whispered from the door of the garage.

Wishbone pointed his muzzle in the direction of the head, and he barked for emphasis.

**119**

Sam walked over to the pile of boxes. "What in the world did you—"

Wishbone knew by the shocked expression on her face that she had sighted the stolen head.

Sam picked up the Bulldog head as if it were the most treasured object in the world. "Oh, Wishbone! You saved the day! You practically handed me this head on a silver platter!"

Wishbone said modestly, "Hey, I'm not such a bad detective *myself.*"

Suddenly, there was a low whirring noise. The garage door began closing electronically.

"Uh-oh!" Wishbone cried out. "Time to scram, Sam!"

As Sam carried the head in both hands, she and Wishbone dashed out of the garage. Seconds later, Wishbone heard the front door of the house open, then close. Next, he heard footsteps trampling after Sam and himself.

"Hurry!" Sam yelled, as she and Wishbone tore like mad down the street. "I'm afraid this guy may not be too happy we stole back the stolen head. For now, let's just get out of here. We'll worry about my bike later."

At the end of the block, two houses down from the Rosenbaums', Wishbone saw the street give way to a section of woods that seemed to be public property. He figured this was a great place for him and Sam to find cover and safety. He gave a bark, and Sam seemed to understand.

"This way!" she cried, running into the street. The hard concrete pounded against Wishbone's paws as he followed Sam toward the woods, and soon they plunged into the thick foliage.

Wishbone knew someone, or something, was still in hot pursuit. It was survival time. As the ground flew by, the dog heard his paws crunching and crackling over the fallen leaves. He thought he also heard his heart slamming back and forth in his chest.

*I definitely like chasing things a lot more than I like being chased.*

Within moments, Wishbone heard the pursuer's feet trampling the leaves a short distance back. He whipped his head around to see who exactly was there. His heart somersaulted with fear. The pursuer was a humongous creature with glaring eyes and terrifyingly sharp teeth.

Wishbone realized he and Sam were being chased by a gigantic bobcat!

*Wait! It's not exactly a real bobcat. It's a . . . What is it?!*

# Chapter Fifteen

As Sam ran through the woods, she suddenly noticed that Wishbone was no longer beside her. Looking over her shoulder, she saw him standing a short way back.

Sam stopped, peering through the trees to see what the dog was eyeing. Her mouth dropped open as she took in the sight of a giant bobcat tearing through the woods. The creature was over five feet tall, and it ran clumsily on two legs. It was obviously a costume, even though it was in much better condition than the Bulldog outfit. As the bobcat came closer, Sam could see it had a body of tan fur, green eyes, long whiskers, and a set of sharp teeth.

Suddenly, she remembered that Jefferson Middle School's mascot was the Bobcat. Then she realized that Mr. Rosenbaum's son must be the one inside the costume. Sensing the situation had reversed from threatening to ridiculous, Sam went over to Wishbone.

"It's an awfully big cat," she said, kneeling to give the dog a few soothing strokes. "But somehow I don't think it's going to hurt us."

Soon the Bobcat stopped a few feet from Sam, glaring at her with its fierce feline eyes.

Sam stood up, glaring right back with her own pair of hazel eyes. "Off with your head!" she ordered.

With its furry paws, the Bobcat lifted its head upward. Sam found herself face to face with Johnny, the boy with the shaggy hair and earring whom she had met at Pepper Pete's on Saturday evening. Sam stood there, holding the Bulldog head, looking at Johnny, who stood there holding the Bobcat head.

"Hi," Johnny said, showing his crooked tooth. "Good to see you again."

Sam thought of her previous conversation with Johnny. She remembered he had told her that he sometimes assisted his dad at work, just as she did. Sam realized that if she had been a more skillful detective, she might have made the connection to Johnny sooner. All the same, she told herself, she had done a pretty good job of catching up with her prey.

In a tone far from friendly, Sam said, "Hi, Johnny."

"You remembered my name," Johnny said, as if nothing of great importance were taking place.

"I also know that you're the Jefferson Bobcat— and that you're a thief."

"So how did you know it was me who stole the head?"

"I had some assistance from Mr. Carr."

"What do you mean? Did I leave some kind of clue at the car?"

"No. I'm referring to the author, John Dickson Carr. Read one of his books, and then maybe you'll understand."

Sam was angry, and Johnny could see it. He nervously ran a hand through his hair. "Listen, Sam. Please give me a chance to explain everything. Can I sit down with you?"

After considering this request for a moment, Sam sat on the ground, leaning against a tree trunk. Johnny sat nearby, looking a bit comical in his costume. After both kids set down their mascot heads, Sam motioned to Wishbone. "Come on, boy, you're part of this, too."

Keeping his eyes on the headless Bobcat, Wishbone walked over to Sam. "Okay," he said, "now I get the full picture. This isn't a 'Hollow Man.' It's a 'Hollow Bobcat.' With a kid inside. I should have realized it sooner, but all this gopher nonsense has made me a little jumpy."

Wishbone sat in the leaves right beside Sam. He wanted to make sure she was all right. He also wanted to see what the phony Bobcat, whom he recognized from Pepper Pete's, had to say for himself.

"Let me start by saying that I've never stolen anything before in my life," Johnny told Sam. "Until Saturday, that is."

"What happened Saturday?" Wishbone and Sam asked at the same time.

Johnny picked up a leaf and fiddled with it as he spoke. "I sometimes help my dad around the shop, and he shows me the tricks of the trade. I never go out alone on a call to install or pick locks. But Saturday was different."

"Why?" Sam asked.

"Jefferson didn't have a football game," Johnny continued, "so I spent the day with Dad. Then, around four-thirty, we got a call for this real simple lock-picking job. I asked Dad if I could do it myself. He said no, that I wasn't ready yet to do a job by myself, but I did my best to convince him that I could do it alone. I guess I wanted to prove myself. Finally, Dad said okay."

"Then what?" Wishbone asked.

"I biked over with the tool bag. I guess it was in your neck of the woods, because it was near Sequoyah Middle School. I did that locksmith job like a real pro. Then I called Dad, gave him the good news, and he told me to have a snack on him. So I biked over to Pepper Pete's. I had my tool bag when I was sitting there, but I guess you didn't see it, because it was under the table."

"Then I waited on you," Sam mentioned. "Very nicely, I might add."

"Yes, you were nice. And I liked you right away. But . . ."

"But what?"

"Yeah, but what?" Wishbone added.

"Around the time I got my pizza," Johnny said, "you stopped waitressing and sat down with your friends. I was keeping an eye on you. Then, for some reason, you lifted your glass and made a toast to 'Toby, the greatest school mascot . . .'"

"I just wanted to make Toby feel better," Sam said abruptly. "But I guess that really bugged you, because you're the Jefferson Bobcat. Naturally, you must consider *yourself* to be the greatest school mascot."

Johnny played a brief drumroll on his leg with his fingers. "Well, yeah, it did spark my sense of school rivalry. But, you see, the Jefferson football team is on this winning streak and it's got the whole school feeling kind of cocky. And me, well, I'm a little cocky to start with. At least that's what my dad says."

"Go on," Sam said.

"Anyway," Johnny said, "I finished my pizza, waved to you, and left. And that should have been the end of it. Except—"

"Except you stole the head," Wishbone put in.

"I was walking through the parking lot to the lamppost where my bike was chained," Johnny continued. "Then I saw this big Bulldog head sitting in the backseat of a sport utility vehicle. I went for a closer look and, remembering your toast to Toby, I realized it was the head of the Sequoyah Bulldog."

"So you stole it," Sam said.

"Now, wait," Johnny said, holding up a hand. "It's not that simple. You have to understand that I was feeling all this school spirit. And I was really psyched about doing that job so well for Dad. And I had the tool bag, which contained the car-lock rods, right there in my hand—"

"So you stole the head," Sam insisted.

"I knew that we were going to have the game with Sequoyah the very next week. It's just . . . how do I put this? Well, the opportunity seemed too perfect to pass up."

"So you stole the head," Sam said again.

"You know, I wasn't even sure I'd be able to get inside the car. The only car I'd practiced picking locks on was my dad's, and I could tell this one would be much more difficult."

"So you stole the head!" Sam declared loudly.

Wishbone backed her up with a resounding bark.

"So I stole the Bulldog head," Johnny confessed. "I picked out the right rod, slithered it down inside the frame of the door, fiddled around a few seconds, and—presto!—the lock lifted and the door opened. I probably wouldn't be able to do it that fast again in a hundred years, but right then I felt this major sense of power. Anyway, after I slipped the head out, I relocked the door, got on my bike, and pedaled home. Then I hid the head in the garage."

"Aha! The truth is revealed!" Wishbone proclaimed. "You know, Sam, maybe you and I should open our own Private Eye detective agency!"

Dusk was now creeping into the woods, changing the area into a world of lengthening shadows. Through the gloom, Sam kept her eyes on Johnny. He glanced down at his Bobcat head, and Sam could see that he was finally feeling some shame for his misdeed.

"I shouldn't have taken that head," Johnny admitted, "even though I had every intention of giving it back to you guys—after the Jefferson–Sequoyah game on Saturday."

"But when you heard the doorbell ring and saw me standing there, you realized I had come for the head," Sam said. "Then, figuring you'd have a last bit of fun with me, you put on your Bobcat costume and tried to trap me and Wishbone in the garage. When we got away, you started chasing us."

"Yes," Johnny said. "And . . . uh . . . well . . . I'm almost afraid to tell you this, but . . . I was also the Jefferson Ghost."

"What!" Sam exclaimed.

"Right after school today," Johnny said, "I met with the cheerleaders to discuss this week's pep rally. When the meeting ended, I left the room. Then, just by chance, I saw you and your friends in the classroom talking to the custodian. I figured you must be on the trail of the missing Bulldog head, so I listened at the door."

Sam spoke sharply. "And when you heard what we were discussing, you saw another opportunity *too perfect to pass up*."

"That's right," Johnny said with some embarrassment. "As soon as I heard you were going to Room two-oh-six to check on that ghost, I ran up a flight of steps and picked my way into the room with a pocket knife. The school has crummy locks. Then I twisted all the lights out of place, picked my way into the classroom next door, and then dashed into the closet. But, Sam, I promise you, this whole thing was in the spirit of fun."

Sam petted Wishbone's head, mostly to keep herself from getting angry again. "I know," she said. "I like to have fun as much as anybody else. But you took the situation way too far, Johnny. Maybe not so much with the ghost thing, but breaking into a car is against the law. You know, Mrs. Talbot could have you arrested if she wanted to. She's the person who owns that car."

A breeze rustled the trees, sending a flurry of leaves downward. "You know what that bag of tools is like?" Johnny said after a thoughtful pause. "What's that ancient myth about—"

"Pandora's box," Sam said, finishing Johnny's thought.

"Yeah. Pandora's Box. The lady is warned not to open it, but she thinks there's all these fabulous things inside. Then when she does open it, all sorts of evil creatures jump out and invade the world and cause terrible things to happen. Those tools can do some good, but they can also do a lot of damage. But then I guess I shouldn't blame the tools. I was the one using them."

"That's right," Sam said.

Johnny crumpled a leaf in his hand. Then he looked at Sam and said, almost pleading, "I want to make this up to you—somehow."

"Forget it," Sam said, looking away.

"No! I really want to do something," Johnny insisted. "Hey! How about if I do an overhaul job on your bike, and the bikes of everyone else who was affected by this mess that I created? I'm really good with bikes. I get them running better than when they were brand-new. Also, I'd like to apologize to Mrs. Talbot."

Sam glanced at her hand. "Well, maybe that would be all right."

"And I'll tell you what else I'll do," Johnny said, getting on his knees to face Sam. "At the game Saturday, at halftime, I'll run over and give the Bulldog a high five. Call it a peace offering."

Sam met Johnny's eyes. "That would be a nice gesture." Johnny revealed his crooked tooth with a relieved smile. Then he picked up the Bulldog head and said, "So I guess you're pretty good friends with this Toby kid who plays the Bulldog."

"We're friends."

"How does he like being the Sequoyah Bulldog?"

Sam caught sight of the Bulldog's sagging eye. Now that she had solved one problem, she began clearly seeing a solution to a couple of other problems.

Sam sprang to her feet. "As a matter of fact," she said, "he hates the job!"

# Chapter Sixteen

By Saturday, fine weather had arrived back in town. Bright and blue and cool, just the way autumn ought to be.

Wishbone lay smack in the middle of Wanda's front yard savoring every inch of a favorite bone. He figured he had a good twenty minutes of chew time left before he had to set off for the afternoon's football game.

Earlier in the week, on Tuesday, Wanda had released several gopher snakes in her front yard. Since then, Wishbone hadn't seen a single trace of his gopher foe. The dog had spent the next few days gathering new bones to replace the ones that were permanently out of reach. Now there was nothing left to do but enjoy.

*This bone is so divinely delicious,* Wishbone thought as he gnawed. *I might just chew it all the way down to the . . . well . . . bone.*

Wishbone heard a slight rustling in the grass. Right behind him. He turned, but he saw nothing. Just the green blades swaying in the breeze.

*Hmm . . . must have been one of those new gopher snakes. I haven't actually seen one yet. I suppose at some point we should introduce ourselves. I assume they don't bother dogs. If they did, they'd probably be called "gopher and dog snakes." Or maybe "general-purpose terrorist snakes." No, I'm sure those snakes will leave me and my bones in perfect peace.*

Sam watched the football slide wildly across the field. A fumble was loose. A player in the scarlet jersey of Jefferson pounced on the ball but it squirted away. A player in the blue-and-gold uniform of Sequoyah scooped up the ball, then spun around and made a mad dash toward the Jefferson goal line.

Along with most everyone else, Sam leaped up to watch the play. "Go, Bulldogs!" she yelled.

"Run that ball!" Joe shouted.

"All the way!" David cheered.

The Sequoyah player made it to the Jefferson thirty-yard line before being tackled.

As Sam sat down, she noticed Wishbone on the bench, happily wagging his tail. "It's funny," she told Joe and David, "but it's almost as if Wishbone understands this game."

"Yeah, right," David said with a scoff. "And maybe the Jefferson Ghost is here, too."

"Hey," Sam said, raising an eyebrow, "you never know."

"At least, I *hope* he's not here," Joe added. "We're tied at seven with the mighty Jefferson team, and we're just about to score another touchdown. I'd hate to see the ghost turn the tide against us."

"If you think the game is good," Sam said, "check out the match between the mascots."

Across the field the Jefferson Bobcat was creeping stealthily along the sidelines, now and then tearing at the air with his claws. Not to be outdone, the Sequoyah Bulldog was prowling the other sideline, growling in a menacing manner and, every once in a while, giving a ferocious lunge. The Bulldog looked fantastic. Not only had Sam repaired both of his eyes, his ears, and his teeth, but she had perked up the nose a bit, too.

"The Bulldog looks like a whole new man," David told Sam.

"It sure does," Joe agreed, "even though it's not really a man."

"Well, thanks," Sam replied, adopting a modest manner. "The whole thing was really no trouble at all."

Joe and David laughed. Monday night Sam had filled them in on all the details of the Bulldog situation, and both boys knew that solving the mystery of the missing mascot head and repairing it was *a great deal of trouble*.

After another three plays, Sequoyah scored a touchdown. Soon afterward, the game broke for halftime. Within minutes, the Sequoyah band was marching up and down the field in formation, blaring, blowing, and drumming away on their instruments. This week there was a new feature to their act. For the opening number, the Bulldog joined the band, performing a fun and funky "Bulldog dance." The crowd cheered and stomped and clapped, loving every sensational second of it. Sam looked at Wishbone and was almost certain that she saw the dog tapping his paw to the music.

"The Bulldog Boogie!" Joe exclaimed.

"Hey, take a look!" David said, pointing.

Sam saw the Jefferson Bobcat dashing over to the Sequoyah Bulldog. When he got there, the Bobcat gave the Bulldog a high five, and then they switched paws

for another high five. The crowd went wild with approval. Sam smiled with satisfaction.

Feeling a tap on her shoulder, Sam turned to see Toby standing behind her. He looked better than Sam had ever seen him. His hair was combed, and even his braces seemed to gleam in the sun. Toby leaned in toward Sam and muttered something.

"I'm sorry," Sam said. "What did you say?"

"I just wanted to thank you again," Toby said, louder.

"Oh, I didn't do much."

"On the contrary," Toby said, "you did a lot. You worked things out with me and Amanda. Then you arranged for the principal to make a speech at Friday's pep rally, announcing that Amanda would be taking over the role of the Bulldog. You even made sure the speech said, 'due to Toby O'Shaughnessy's other commitments,' so I could save face. Now I can focus my energy on things more important to me, like my science projects. You know, I think my atom display has a real shot at the regional finals this year. Anyway, Sam, I really appreciate all you've done."

"I think my timing was good, too," Sam said, watching the Bulldog resume her crowd-pleasing dance. "Because of the Bulldog job, Amanda foamed at the mouth only a tiny bit when she learned Crystal got the lead in the winter play."

Toby gave Sam a pat on the back, then walked away happily.

"Some folks just aren't cut out to be dogs," Wishbone said, as he watched Toby stroll down the bleachers. "Even so, that Toby is an awfully nice kid." Then Wishbone noticed the Jefferson Bobcat standing on the twenty-yard line, giving a friendly wave to him and Sam.

Blushing with embarrassment, Sam waved back at the Bobcat. She had come to realize Johnny Rosenbaum wasn't such a bad guy after all. A few days before, Johnny had called Mrs. Talbot to apologize, and he also made sure she knew he had confessed his crime to his dad, who grounded him for three weeks. Even without the punishment, Sam felt sure Johnny wouldn't be stealing any more mascot heads or anything else.

"Sam," David said, putting a hand on her shoulder, "you've proven yourself the master of the impossible. Against all odds, you solved the mystery of the missing Bulldog head. Then you brought the head back to life and found a way to put it on just the right person. Now, thanks to you, everyone is happy."

After flashing his great smile, Joe said, "And who knows? Our team is so pumped up, I think we may just win this game!"

"Well," Sam remarked, "I've learned something this past week. If you put your mind to it, few things in life are truly impossible! Don't you agree, Wishbone?"

"I certainly do," Wishbone said, looking up fondly at Sam. "Or, as Dr. Gideon Fell himself might say, 'H'mf, ha!'"

# About Alexander Steele

Alexander Steele is a writer of books, plays, and screen-plays for both youngsters and adults—and some-times for dogs. *Tale of the Missing Mascot* is his first book for the WISHBONE Mysteries series. He is also writing *Moby Dog* for The Adventures of Wishbone series.

Mystery and history are favorite subjects of Alexander's. He has written seven detective novels for young readers. Currently, he is working on a novel for adults that explores the origin of detectives in both fiction and reality.

Among the plays that Alexander has penned is the award-winning *One Glorious Afternoon*. The story line fo-cuses on Shakespeare and his fellow players at the Globe Theatre, in London.

Alexander became very interested in John Dickson Carr while preparing this current book. Carr considered the mystery story "the grandest game in the world," and he wrote almost a hundred of them. His stories run the gamut in tone from ghostly to comic to historical. The vast majority of them, however, fall into the "locked-room" category. Carr is the master of the locked-room mystery, and it is astonishing how many variations he composed on this theme. Alexander hopes that *Tale of the Missing Mascot* would have both pleased and puzzled John Dickson Carr.

Alexander lives in New York City, where there is no shortage of locked doors . . . or mysteries behind them.

# WHAT HAS FOUR LEGS, A HEALTHY COAT, AND A GREAT DEAL ON MEMBERSHIP?

## IT'S THE WISHBONE ZONE™
### THE OFFICIAL WISHBONE™ FAN CLUB!

When you enter the **WISHBONE ZONE,** you get:
- Color poster of **Wishbone**™
- **Wishbone** newsletter filled with photos, news, and games
- Autographed photo of **Wishbone** and his friends
- **Wishbone** sunglasses, and more!

To join the fan club, pay $10 and charge your **WISHBONE ZONE** membership to VISA, MasterCard, or Discover. Call:

### 1-800-888-WISH

Or send us your name, address, phone number, birth date, and a check for $10 payable to Big Feats! (TX residents add $.83 sales tax/IN residents add $.50 sales tax). Write to:

### WISHBONE ZONE
P.O. Box 9523
Allen, TX 75013-9523

Prices and offer are subject to change. Place your order now!

# Now Playing on Your VCR...

## Two exciting **WISHBONE** stories on video!

Ready for an adventure? Then leap right in with **Wishbone**™ as he takes you on a thrilling journey through two great action-packed stories. First, there are haunted houses, buried treasure, and mysterious graves in two back-to-back episodes of *A Tail in Twain*, starring **Wishbone** as Tom Sawyer. Then, no one is more powerful than **Wishbone**, in *Hercules Unleashed*, featuring exciting new footage! It's more fun than a flea dip! It's **Wishbone** on home video.

**WISHBONE**™

Available wherever videos are sold.

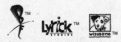